Lie Down in the Ashes

KATY L. WOOD

All rights reserved. Published in the United States by Aspen & Copper Publishing. Special hardback edition published 2025.

www.AspenAndCopper.com

Hello@AspenAndCopper.com

Educators, librarians, and others interested in arranging an appearance by Katy L. Wood at their event should contact her at the above provided e-mail.

Summary: When five friends go camping before the start of their senior year, they're expecting a fun night of relaxing in the woods they've grown up in, but after months of dangerous drought the forest is tinder dry. One member of the group doesn't care, though, and lights a campfire anyway. A single gust of wind is all it takes for the fire to spiral out of control. Up at the nearby mine, the miners witness the start of the fire and debate what to do with the old retired fire equipment they use, but two of them decide not to wait for a decision from the others and steal the trucks.

Kickstarter Special Edition Hardback ISBN: N/A
Hardback ISBN: --
Paperback ISBN: --
EBook ISBN: --

Little Disaster Books are short standalone novels, each featuring a different disaster, lots of queer characters, a focus on hope, and endings that don't stop with the rescue, because sometimes the hardest part to survive is the after.

Learn more at www.AspenAndCopper.com/LittleDisasterBooks.

LIE DOWN IN THE ASHES

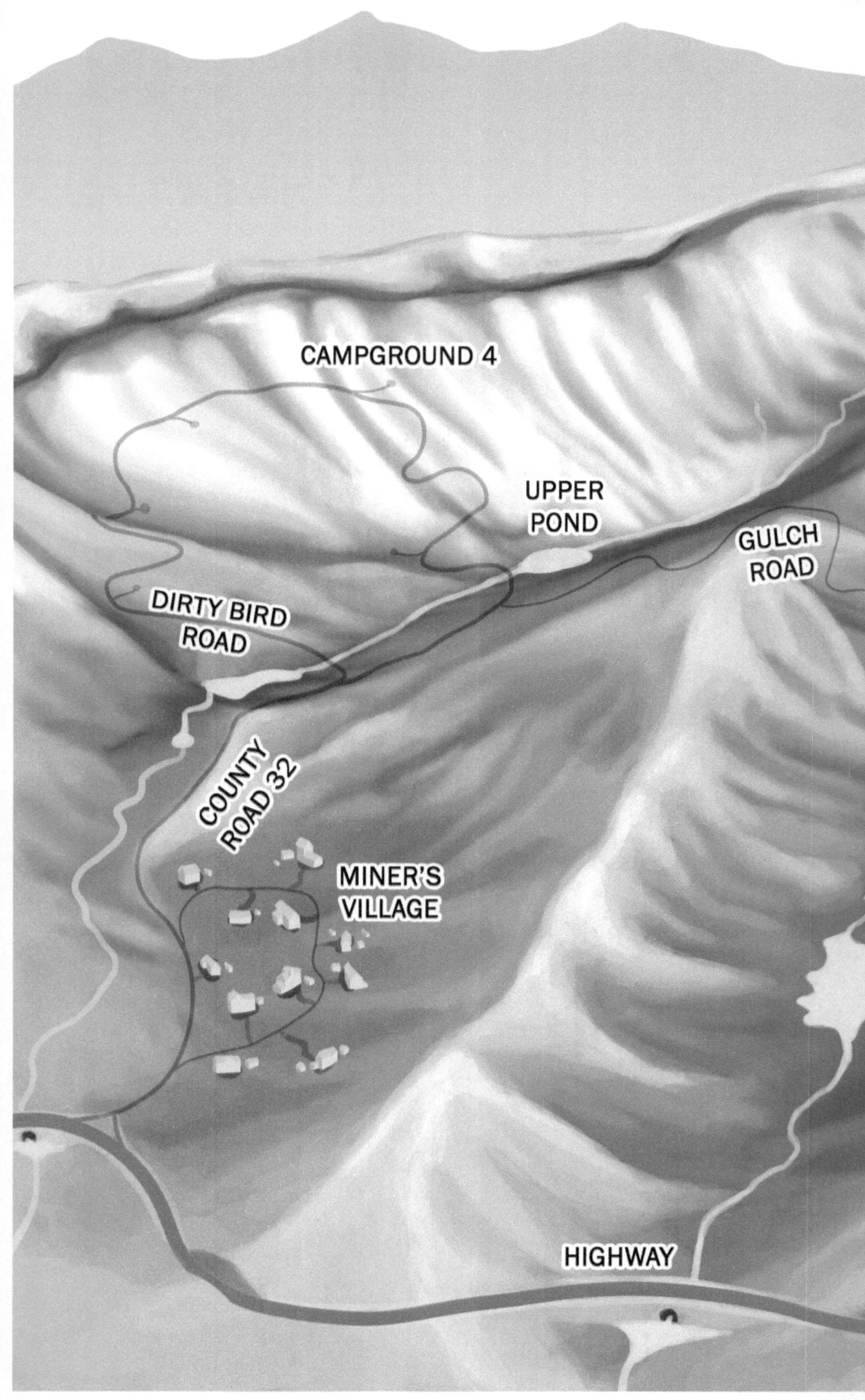

CAMPGROUND 4
UPPER
POND
GULCH
ROAD
DIRTY BIRD
ROAD
COUNTY
ROAD 32
MINER'S
VILLAGE
HIGHWAY

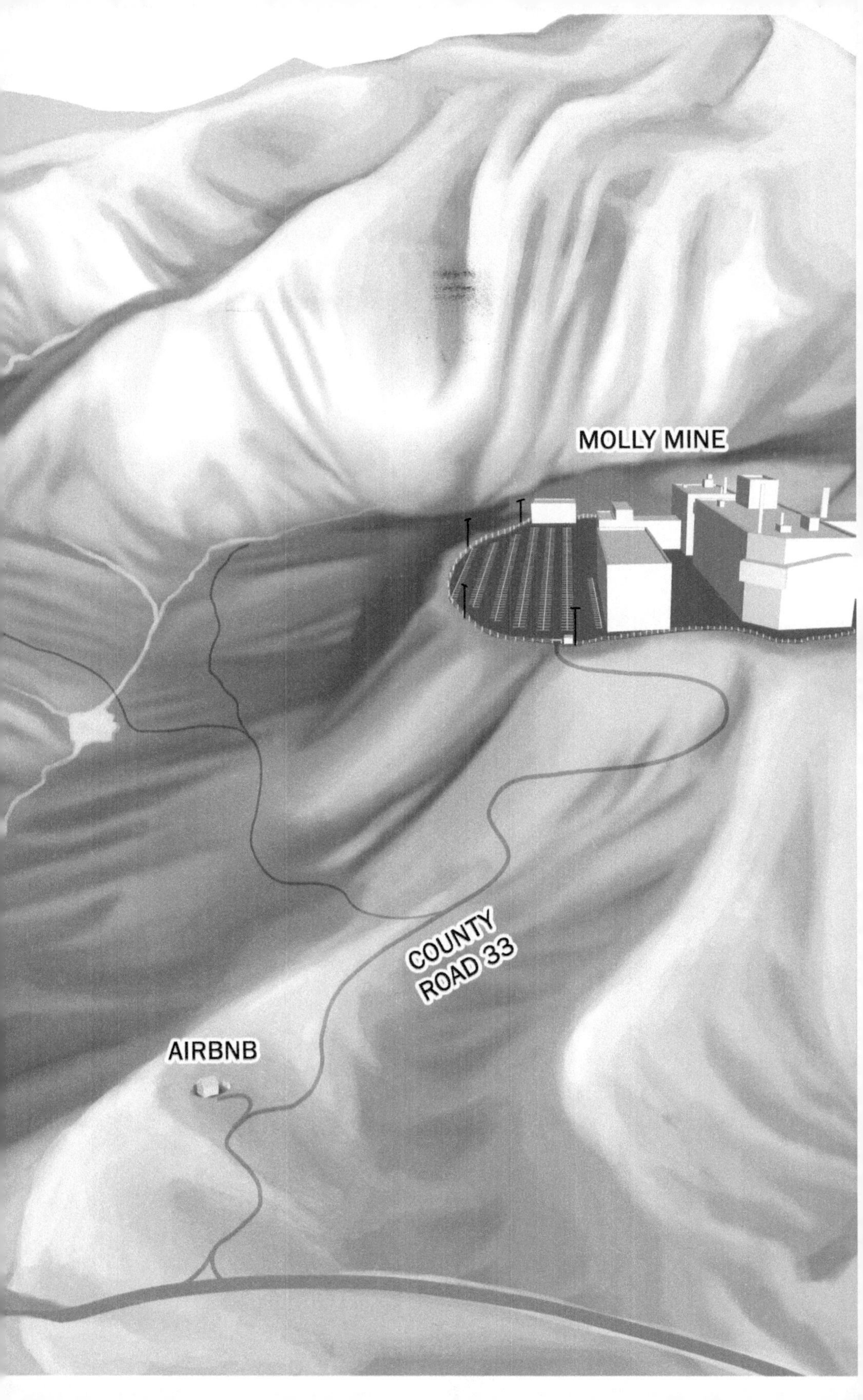

MOLLY MINE
COUNTY ROAD 33
AIRBNB

For the helpers.

AUGUST 2019

CHAPTER 1: CAMPOUT

River

After a long morning and a good portion of the afternoon under the baking August sun, our garage smelled heavily of warm dirt, oil, and hot metal. It was almost pleasant, the heat and scents all soaking into my senses as I stared out at the view from the open door, mountains stretching from horizon to horizon. Or it would have been pleasant, had I not been running so far behind.

Should I have changed the oil in my truck anytime other than an hour before my camping trip? Yes. Had I? No. Four friends to pick up all over our little town of Sadie's Hill and yet here I was, slamming down a concoction of coffee and Redbull, tossing my hair up into a bun, and hoping to break some oil change records. Cursing my poor planning, I crawled under my ancient red Ford with a wrench and a bucket to catch the old oil. I had to go in a bit sideways to avoid the winch on the bumper, wiggling my shoulders and dragging the oil tray along until I was in position. A long blond hair greeted me, tickling against my face from where it was caught on the old oil filter. What an intrepid little strand, clinging on down here since I'd last changed the oil. I knew I'd bottomed the truck out at least twice since my last change, yet there it was.

"River?" My dad's voice said from somewhere near my feet.

"Hang on, don't make me drop oil on my face," I responded, pulling my arm up and into position to loosen the drain plug. Oil splooshed out, a few drops splattering onto my face before I made it out of the way.

"You coulda asked me, sweetheart," my dad said as I started to wiggle my way back out.

"'Your truck, your responsibility,'" I parroted. "That was what you said when I bought this instead of the newer Subaru you wanted me to get."

He sighed dramatically. "It was a nice Subaru, baby girl."

I rolled my eyes, giving him a playful shove with my shoulder as I went to peruse our rack of car fluids for a jug of my oil and a new filter. Probably should've done that first. If I was this scatterbrained now, school in a week would be a nightmare.

"It was green," my dad continued.

"Green is your favorite color, not mine." I pawed through the jugs, finally locating two of the right brand way at the back. One was full, the other not quite. I shook it, listening to the fluid slosh around inside. Meh. Enough for the weekend. I could get more when I got paid next week and top it off. "Besides, the Subaru sat too low. It would've gotten caught in snow drifts." Snow drifts were the least of my worries when it came to going over things I shouldn't. "And it didn't have a winch." A bit more pawing revealed a filter.

"Do you even *use* the winch?"

Yes. More than he ever needed to know. It was very useful for hauling friends out of the ditch at three a.m. before the cops arrived to chew us out for drag racing down the two-mile, mostly straight stretch of two-lane highway on the east side of town. Or for hauling myself out of the same situation. I never won, not in my old tank, but plenty of the farm kids had trucks that were just as old or older. Winning at least felt like a possibility until the shift into fourth gear when things started making alarming grinding noises. I really needed to get that checked. It was beyond my meager mechanicing abilities.

"Where you kids headed this time?" my dad asked.

"Up to Lost Hen," I told him, plopping back onto the concrete to retrieve the tray of old oil, change the filter, and close everything up. "Not sure which campground we'll stop at."

"Well, be safe. Don't park on the dry grass, and remember there's still a full fire ban."

You'd never know I'd been born and raised here the way he talked. It *was* dry, though. "I know, I know."

"Bring your safety matches."

"Yes, sir."

"And plenty of water."

"Always."

"There's supposed to be some wind tonight, too."

"Got it."

The town fire station shimmered in the heat when I pulled up to the curb. Half the crew was lazing outside in shady spots with their lunches, enjoying the weather. Our tiny station in our equally tiny town averaged a grand total of one call every two days—most of them for traffic accidents—and *maybe* one serious one every month. As for actual fires, they tended to only see a handful every year, up until recently. Still, it was usually just someone's kitchen or a single tree that had been hit by lightning and smoldered for a few days before someone noticed. This made for a lot of very skilled firefighters who had almost nothing to do but train and show off their trucks to the local kids. One of my best friends, Dante, was more than happy to use this to his advantage, sneaking in as much training as he could before he turned eighteen and could officially join. He was there now, light brown skin turned even warmer over the summer and with a smile just as warm as he talked with several of the crew members.

"Suck uuuupppp," I called, dangling out my driver's side window.

Dante rolled his eyes, flipping me off with a smile. His black cargo pants were soaked, a casualty of washing the engines as part of his helping out at the station. Engine 41 sat there, gleaming brightly, sunlight sparking off the chrome detailing. Dante had done a good job, I'd give him that.

Waving goodbye to the several firefighters milling around, he retrieved his pack from inside and tossed it into the bed of my truck before climbing in the backseat.

"See you Monday?" one of the firefighters, Peter, called.

"Yep! In the afternoon, after practice. See ya, Peter!" Dante answered.

"See ya." Peter waved. Even as a lesbian I couldn't help but marvel at his well-defined arms.

I grinned at Dante in the rearview mirror. "Question, are you really volunteering because you want to join up, or just for the access to a lot of nice, muscled men?"

Dante grinned back. "There are many benefits to being a firefighter."

Cackling, I pulled us back onto the road to pick up the rest of our friends, heading to Iris's place first. She lived with her parents and brother behind her father's mechanic shop and was waiting on her porch when I pulled up. Her little brother, six years younger than her, was there too, laughing at something she'd said. She gave him a sloppy kiss on the cheek that made him scrunch up his face in annoyance that I knew was just pretend.

Dante got out to help Iris with her stuff, giving her brother a fistbump before taking the cooler she indicated and putting it in the bed. Iris added a tent and a bag full of other gear. She and Dante slid into the backseat, Iris cramming her ever-present, excessively large, and over-stickered water bottle under the seat. Once settled, she gave Dante a kiss, snuggling into his side. Dante looked at her with a stupidly happy little grin that brought out the dimple on his left cheek. They looked good together, him in his comfortably worn flannel and her in her self-embroidered denim overalls and wonderfully horrible paisley t-shirt, both of them glowing with summer tans, though she was still much paler than his warm brown.

Last stop was Toby and Natalie who, conveniently, lived right across the street from one another on the outskirts of town. Their houses couldn't be more different, though. Natalie lived in a rundown little ranch house that was only about a thousand square feet. It sat on two acres, though, giving her plenty of room to garden and keep some chickens and goats for 4H. Toby, on the other hand, lived in a custom built six-thousand square foot, sprawling log home. The whole thing looked like it had popped out of a catalog, kitschy moose and pinecone decor and all. No one was quite sure where his family's money came from, but they had a lot of it and there were plenty of rumors despite his family living in town for over fifteen years now. The more down to earth rumors involved things like inheritances and stocks. The wilder ones involved drug smuggling and espionage, and tended to only come up when people were drunk and bored. Toby always blew the questions off, though, insisting he was just like everyone else and money didn't matter, so why talk about it? An easy thing to say when you were the one with the money.

Natalie and Toby were waiting together, sitting with their gear on an artfully mossy stone wall that marked the entrance to Toby's driveway. At least once a month the landscapers were out there with spray bottles of blended up moss water to keep the effect in place. Natalie had one daypack next to her, covered in patches from local parks and a few sewn-up rips. Toby had what looked like half an REI store. A huge tent bag, two coolers, a big camp chair, a sixty-liter backpacking bag—complete overkill for a trip that would require zero hiking—massive sleeping bag, two pillows, and an additional duffle bag.

More and more lately, I'd been getting annoyed at Toby's inability to not wave his wealth around in people's faces. When we were kids, he'd just been the guy with all the cool toys. Now he was the teenager spending the money himself, and acting like that made him important.

Tamping down my annoyance, I pulled up in front of him and Natalie. He was like a brother to her, after all. I could put up with him for the weekend.

Toby jumped up, throwing his arms wide. "Finally!"

"Oh hush," I said as the truck rolled to a stop. "It's only sixish, we've got plenty of daylight left."

"Yeah but I wanna goooo," Toby said, tossing his shiny gear haphazardly into the bed before jumping into the remaining backseat.

Natalie smiled and shook her head, tucking her gear into the bed and making sure it was secure, as well as securing Toby's, before sliding into the passenger seat.

"Hi, baby." I grinned.

"Hi, baby." Natalie grinned back.

We leaned over the center console and I tangled a hand into her hair to pull her in for a kiss.

"Come ooooonnnn," Toby said from the backseat, bouncing up and down enough to make the truck shake. Dante reached around Iris and swatted at him, but Toby dodged out of the way with a laugh.

I pulled away enough for only Natalie to see me roll my eyes. She made a guiltily but amused face and shrugged.

Sighing, I gave her another quick kiss, then sat back in my seat. "Let the camping weekend commence!"

"It is just cruel to start school when the world is still this lovely outside," Natalie said. She had one arm dangling out the window of my truck, rolling her pale, freckled hand up and down through the wind. Blue sky spread out above us, not a cloud to be seen. The scents of sage and pine were almost overwhelming. Everything was just starting to take on the burnished gold quality that meant fall would be coming soon.

I smiled, taking my hand off the gearshift for a moment to reach over and tuck a stray strand of chestnut hair behind her ear. "Last year, at least."

"Speak for yourselves. Lucky senior bastards," Iris piped up from the backseat. She was practically seated on Dante's lap, and it made me smile. I was glad Iris managed to find someone who cared about her as much as Dante did. The dating pool in our small mountain town was hardly a deep one even if you weren't queer. As far as I knew, we were the only queer people at all in our school, which was a big part of why we stuck together, even as Toby grew more and more obnoxious with age.

"I, for one, am looking forward to our return to the halls of education," Toby said. He too had his arm dangling out an open window, but rather than rolling it through the wind he was tapping the flaking red door along with the beat of the bluegrass song that was crackling over the old radio.

"You're just looking forward to pulling senior pranks!" Dante laughed. "How long is your list of plans now?"

"Forty-two objectives," Toby grinned. "Stage one involves goats."

"You are not using my goats, Toby!" Natalie said.

"Or mine!" I added. Neil and Sally were my babies. They were meant to be 4H goats a few years ago, except they'd never sold because Neil was born with a deformed back leg and Sally was blind, and they didn't have a single braincell between them. Cliff? Walk off it. Glass? Walk into it. Food trough moved a foot to the right? Didn't exist anymore. Sun went down? World ended, better scream about it.

"Ladies, ladies, the goats will be fine! Principal Davidson's office, on the other hand...."

"No, Toby!" Everyone said at once before dissolving into fits of laughter.

Half-an-hour after leaving town, we swung north onto the turnoff for County Road 32, trundling past Miner's Village. It was just a smattering of a dozen houses between two ridges, more a neighborhood than anything, but everyone called it Miner's Village since it was mostly occupied by people who worked at the mine on the next ridge to the east. At least three of the houses had been converted into bunk houses with a dozen or more miners staying in each. The legalities of this were mostly treated as a don't ask, don't tell situation by the county.

A group of kids on their bikes raced into our dust trail, waving at us as they did. Iris twisted around and slid open the back window, hanging out it to wave back and make faces at them.

This felt good. A last camping weekend with the gang before school set in and stole away all our time. Sure, we'd probably get back together for a hunting season or two, but it would be hard to coordinate all five of us being in one place at once. I had only drawn a doe license for the second rifle season this year, and I didn't know what the others had, or what over-the-counter licenses might be available. Dante would be all over the county, the state even, playing football, volunteer work eating up the rest of his time. Iris had her doctor appointments in the city. Natalie was still flying all over the country to visit colleges. Toby was a wild card, as likely to be home as he was to be jetting off to Jamaica or some other far-flung destination. It made me ache a bit to think about the different paths all our lives were on. Even Toby, as much as he annoyed me, was still a friend, and had been part of my life for as long as I could remember. Hopefully, this would only be the last camping trip of the summer, not our last camping trip ever.

"Here," Natalie said, pulling a hair tie off the collection on her wrist and handing it back to Iris, who was struggling with keeping her hair from blowing into her face now that she was seated again.

"Thanks," Iris said, pulling her shoulder-length black curls back into a messy, semi-functional ponytail. A lot of strands didn't quite make it, though, so she groaned and tried again. "I'm not used to having long hair yet, and I never knew it would be so *curly*. Being a girl is so much unexpected work."

Natalie reached back over the center console and patted Iris's knee. "Yes, yes it is. Welcome to the club. We'll have a hair care lesson when we get home. Get you some good conditioner and satin pillowcases."

Dante took the hair tie and began gently finger-combing Iris's curls into submission for her.

"Satin?" Iris said, face scrunched in confusion.

"Yeah, curly hair is fragile," I said. "You have to baby it."

Or so I was told by Natalie. My hair was stick straight and dirty blond. Natalie, with her bouncy curls, said this was a gift when it came to maintenance.

Iris groaned and slumped back against Dante who wrapped his arms around her shoulders and kissed the top of her head. He'd had much better luck with her ponytail.

"Do I even want to know what annoying experiences boobs are going to bring when the hormones kick in enough for me to get them?" Iris asked.

"Spending all your money on bras," Natalie said.

"Backaches," I said.

Conversation ceased when I turned up Dirty Bird Road, which had gotten rather sloppy over the summer even though it hadn't rained in two months. It was more of a hunter's road than anything, though, so it didn't warrant county maintenance. The only thing allowing it to keep the status of being a road was that people kept stubbornly driving over it despite the pits and ruts.

The truck bounced and jostled along, used to this rough treatment. Maybe a piece or two would fall off, but they wouldn't be the first nor the last. As long as all our stuff stayed in the bed we were good. I upshifted and downshifted, rolling the wheel back and forth beneath my other palm, as we went over one rise, down another, and up again on the next one, steadily gaining altitude the whole way. The truck skidded to a stop at the edge of a clearing near the top of the ridge, the dust catching up and billowing around the cab before blowing away on the breeze. Tall, thin pines loomed up around us, swaying and sending their shadows dancing over the camp spot I'd picked.

"We have arrived," I declared, putting the truck into park.

Toby whooped and threw himself out of the car, skipping around the clearing, kicking away fallen sticks and pinecones as he did. Dante and Iris joined him, helping clean up the campsite in a much less chaotic manner.

"He is not borrowing any of our goats," Natalie said, watching Toby through the windshield.

"Not a chance," I agreed, tangling my fingers with Natalie's. Her skin was warm and soft beneath mine, the freckles thick from a summer of working outside in her garden.

"You send in your application for Western yet?" Natalie asked.

I shook my head. I wasn't worried, though. I still wasn't even sure I wanted to go to college. Western just seemed like a good option because, at least if I decided I hated the classes, there were tons of adventure programs offered through the college to keep me busy. Ice climbing and kayaking and spelunking among plenty of others.

The engine ticked away its heat in front of us and I caught

snatches of Iris laughing at something Toby said. Her hair was loose again, the sunlight picking out all the subtle brown tone shifts amongst the black.

"You've got your pensive face on," Natalie said.

I shrugged, watching our friends. Objectively, Dante was growing up to be quite attractive. High cheekbones, eyes and a smile that could convince you to share secrets. Poor Iris was essentially going through a second puberty now that she was on estrogen, but it was starting to soften her face in a lovely way and, as much as her curly hair annoyed her, it suited the oval shape of her face. Toby was still stuck in an awkward, gangly state and no amount of money seemed to be able to tame his mop of brown hair, but I was sure with another few years he'd grow into himself better. Maybe by then he'd get his attitude in check too, but I doubted it.

And Natalie. God, I loved Natalie. Her laugh, the secret little tattoo of a star on her hip, the freckles along her shoulders, the devotion she showed Ben, her brother who had cerebral palsy. Everything about Natalie just *fit* for me. It didn't even sting that Natalie wanted to leave the state for college; I always knew that was coming. She'd decided she would study the stars when she was three and hadn't changed her mind since. We'd find a way to make it work as soon as we knew for sure where she was going.

"Whaaat?" Natalie said, leaning over to rest her chin on my shoulder.

"Just thinking about the future," I replied.

"That isn't allowed this weekend," Natalie said. "This weekend is for now."

"Are you two coming or what?!" Toby shouted at us.

"'For now' is an interesting way to put it," I replied to Natalie. "Bit of a double entendre."

Natalie shrugged, giving me a peck on the cheek. "Come on, before Toby drags us out of here."

With that she slid out of the truck, making the cab jostle, and went around to start pulling gear out of the bed. I tossed the keys onto the dashboard so they wouldn't get lost and followed.

Pausing a moment at my tailgate, I looked out at the view

between the trees. Our patchily forested ridge slipped away down into a little gulch, the bottom filled with sage and scrub before the land rose again to form the next forest-covered ridge to the east. Just beyond that was the mine, but only a sliver of the tallest building and a bunch of antennas could be seen from here, the rest obscured by spindly pines. I took a deep breath, letting the scent of nature fill my lungs. At least if this was going to be our last camping trip, it would be a good one.

"Mighty mountain woman!" Toby shouted, playfully flexing his arms in my direction as I carried two stacked coolers to the area next to the ring of rocks around the empty firepit. I rolled my eyes but wasn't sure Toby caught it as my face was smashed against the top cooler.

Dante and Iris were busying themselves with their tent, trying to figure out the proper arrangement of the supporting rods. The tent was brand new, something Iris received for her birthday back at the beginning of summer. Every trip we'd taken so far, we'd just slept under the stars, so she hadn't used it yet. Clearly, her and Dante wanted a little privacy if the tent was finally making an appearance.

Natalie went to help with the tent as I pulled camping chairs out of their bags and set them up around the coolers. Toby's was indeed rather excessive, with a tall back that could be set at multiple angles, and a footrest that could be folded out. It looked like a throne compared to the ratty chairs the rest of us brought.

"No, I'm pretty sure it is supposed to be, like, an X but with this little rod connecting the two Vs," Iris said, holding the rods aloft to examine them as they flopped around.

"It didn't come with instructions?" Natalie asked.

"Of course it did, but that's boring," Dante replied.

Natalie shook her head and started in on our own tent, a simple red and black one with a regular X of support rods. It had just enough room for two people willing to get cozy, and we were more than willing to get cozy.

A loud clattering sound behind me made me jump and I spun on my heels to see Toby clapping wood shavings and dust off his hands, a pile of wood in the firepit at his feet. It was all gray and baked bone dry; pine that had been on the ground for a couple years, at least.

Dante saw the sticks too and raced over.

"Nope, not a chance. No campfires," he said.

"Oh come ooooon," Toby whined. "Who camps without a campfire?"

"No," Dante said firmly. "There's a full fire ban for a reason."

Toby rolled his eyes. "That's just for the dumb flatlanders who don't know what they're doing and come up to the mountains for the weekend to coo at a bunch of mangy mule deer. We live up here, we know how to have a campfire."

"No," Dante repeated. "It hasn't even sprinkled in months, and we haven't had a good soaking rain since back in spring. No. Campfire."

"Just because you want to be some hotshot smokejumper doesn't mean you're a firefighter yet," Toby said. "Get off your high horse. I want a campfire."

"Hotshots and Smokejumpers are two different things," Dante said, arms crossing. "And it doesn't even matter, because *we are not having a campfire.*"

"But—" Toby started.

"Toby," I interrupted, putting on my best mom voice. I knew where I stood in this group of queer mountain kids. The first to come out to the world at large, the first to feel comfortable in their own skin. It somehow meant I was usually in charge, usually the arbitrator in disagreements. I was okay with that, and didn't mind using it when needed. Especially with Toby.

Toby sighed and slouched off, kicking his sleeping bag towards his still unassembled tent.

"He's going to pout for the rest of the night," Dante muttered.

I shrugged. "Let him. He needs to get used to not always getting his way."

"He won't," Dante replied. "Not with his kind of parents."

"They have kind of spoiled him," I said, casting my eyes sideways to make sure Toby couldn't hear us.

"Kind of? River, they bought him a $40,000 Jeep. And then

they got him another one when he wrecked the first one. $40,000 is almost twice what my mom makes in a *year* working at the County Market, without even counting all the aftermarket crap he's bolted on."

I shrugged. It was nice to know Dante was on my side, but what was there to say? Toby being rich and spoiled was nothing new. Neither was the entitlement that sometimes came from that. He was still our friend.

"You're the one who dated him," I pointed out.

"Yeah, for, like, two months when we were twelve!" Dante said. "Relationships don't count until you're at least fifteen. Before that they're just puppy crushes. Besides, I just wanted to play with his Hot Wheels more. He had, like, five hundred and a whole playroom full of track."

I gave a dramatic gasp, clutching a hand to my chest. "Hot Wheel whore!"

"Hush," he said, swatting my shoulder with a smile.

I snickered and turned to watch Natalie who was leaning into our tent, arranging sleeping mats and bags. The slowly setting sun was turning her brown hair amber with little threads of gold, and I felt something stirring in my gut. I went over, leaning down and reaching into the tent to catch Natalie's chin.

"Come with me," I said with a lopsided grin.

Natalie gave me a little mischievous smile. "Why should I do that?"

"Come with me," I repeated with a gentle tug.

Natalie gave in, standing up and dusting off her pants. Toby wolf-whistled behind us as I led the way out of the clearing, fingers tangling with Natalie's. My other hand was free, though, and I used it to flip Toby off.

CHAPTER 2: IGNITION

Dante

"Having fun in here?" I asked, poking my head into the tent.

Iris smiled from the center of a mess of sleeping bags and stuff she'd pulled out from her bag. "Tons. Kinda lonely though."

"Oh, well, we can't have that." I crawled all the way into the tent and sat across from her.

"So," she said.

"So."

"We're sharing a tent."

"We are indeed," I agreed. "But...if you've changed your mind, that's fine. I'll go steal a spot in Toby's tent, the thing is the size of a small apartment."

She shook her head. "I haven't. Changed my mind, I mean. It's still just...kind of weird, though."

I nodded. "That's fair."

"I never thought I had much dysphoria, not really, but..." she trailed off with a shrug, breaking eye contact and tucking a lock of hair behind her ear.

I gently nudged her knee with my foot. "Everyone gets nervous showing their body to their partner for the first time. Gender has nothing to do with it."

She looked back up at me with a little smile. "What if you do like it now, though, but don't like it after I have surgery?"

"I'll like whatever you look like," I responded. It was true. She was gorgeous no matter what. "Did you ask your parents yet? About surgery?"

She sighed and nodded. "Yeah. They're fine with me getting

it, but they don't want me to use my college fund for it like I asked. I tried to tell them how much easier it would be than fighting with insurance, how I don't even want to go to college anyway, but I didn't get anywhere."

"You've still got two years to win them over," I said, reaching out to wrap her hands up in mine. "And plenty of time to win some big rodeo pot and use that money instead."

"Such faith in my rodeo skills."

"They are very good skills."

She grinned. "Oh really?"

"Mmmhm." I leaned forward and she met me in the middle for a soft kiss. All I wanted was to keep kissing her, but a shout from Toby asking for help with his tent broke us apart.

"I've been summoned," I sighed.

Iris patted my knee. "Someone has to help him set up the apartment."

I rolled my eyes, gave her another quick peck, and crawled back out of the tent. Toby was standing next to a large rectangle of rumpled fabric, a bunch of poles on top of it.

"Aren't you rich enough to afford one that just pops open through some sort of expensive magic?" I asked, leaning down to grab a pole.

"And listen to River call me a glamper? Not a chance."

I didn't point out this tent was still pretty much a glamper tent anyway with its three sections, multiple zip-up windows, and the fact you could stand up inside with room to spare. All it was missing was a bathroom.

Together we threaded the poles into all the right spots and pulled everything taut, erecting the structure in about ten minutes. Toby put his hands on his hips and nodded in satisfaction.

"Thanks. Now...about a campfire."

"No, Toby. Not happening."

"Come on, Dante, just a little one?" Toby tried. "Five sticks. Just enough for marshmallows once the sun goes down."

If Toby didn't drop this soon, I was going to follow Natalie and River's lead and take Iris off into the forest for a real makeout session. Except that would leave Toby unsupervised, which probably wasn't a good idea. More and more, having him around felt like babysitting.

"No," I said. "Stop asking."

"You're not in charge," Toby pointed out.

"No, but I am twice your size and I had the most tackles out of anyone in the county last season. Care to try your luck?"

Toby sized me up for a minute then shook his head.

"Here," Iris said, getting up from where she'd been going through the coolers and putting a beer in Toby's hand. "Occupy your mouth with this instead of talking."

"Iris! Always there for us with the beers," Toby said, hooking an arm over her shoulders and planting a sloppy kiss on her cheek. "Thank you!"

"Happy to provide," Iris said, pulling away to hand me one as well.

"Thanks, love," I said. "Your dad gonna miss them?"

"Nah," Iris replied, taking a sip of her own. "I took them from the beer fridge in the shop. He'll figure his mechanics drank them."

"Naughty, naughty," Toby said, letting out a loud belch.

"You're disgusting," Iris laughed.

"I seem to remember a belching contest last week that you won," I pointed out, grinning at her over the lip of my beer. Her nose scrunched up and she stuck her tongue out at me.

Our relationship was new, only a few months old, but her smile still sent a thrill through me. She was terrifyingly pretty. Always had been. I still remembered the first time I'd seen her at a weekend rodeo one town over, strong thighs gripping the sides of her chocolate-colored mare, Fiddle, as the two of them twisted around barrels. They'd taken the turns so tight Iris's knees almost brushed the ground. I'd known her before that, she'd moved here shortly after my family had ten years earlier, but that rodeo was the first time I'd really *seen* her. I hadn't looked back since, even if it took me almost a year to convince her my feelings were genuine no matter what her gender was.

She could see me thinking about her and blushed, hiding it

behind another sip of beer. We'd stayed up late video chatting the night before, and she'd insisted we share a tent. We had yet to do that. It made the coming night feel both terrifyingly close and achingly far away. Sneaking into one another's beds for a few hours while our parents slept was one thing, but there was something so much more intimate about the enclosed space of a little tent. Not having parents around helped too.

I needed a minute, or I was going to reach a point where my pants gave away my hopes for the night. Not that anything would happen if Iris didn't want it to. I wasn't even sure *I* wanted it to. But certain parts of my anatomy had other ideas.

"Be right back, need to pee," I said, handing Iris my beer.

"Don't get eaten by a cougar," she replied.

"I'll do my best," I told her, trotting off among the trees.

It took some work to get far enough away from camp for privacy, heading down the slope away from the direction that River and Natalie had gone. There were a lot of beetle-killed lodgepole pines littering the ground I had to climb over. They lay tangled together like a giant's game of pick-up sticks, spear sharp branches jutting off in all directions. Raspberry bushes, a couple weeks past ripe, sprouted up where they found room, adding tiny thorns to the mess. There wasn't even really anything to duck behind, the still standing lodgepoles only providing a foot of cover at best as they flexed and swayed in the wind. Any semblance of old growth pine had been logged away long ago.

Finding a place that was good enough, I unzipped my pants, taking a few calming breaths as I did. Everything was fine. Iris and I were just sharing a tent. Just. Sharing a tent. It was fine. Maybe something would happen, maybe it wouldn't. Either way, we were going to have a great night. And then we were going to have another one tomorrow, and then we were going to go home and get ready for school to start in a week.

Zipping back up, I headed for camp, trying to focus on things that weren't sharing a tent with my dangerously pretty girlfriend. The falling evening light casting long shadows across the forest. The tiny chipmunks skittering along the fallen trunks. The fat gray camp robbers hopping among the branches and having twittering arguments with one another. The push and pull of the wind as it came and went. Not Iris's laugh. Not the way she liked to tuck herself against my chest and under my chin. Not the twinkle in her bark-brown eyes when she was up to something. Nope. None of that. Just the forest.

When I made it back to camp, still in much the same anxious condition I'd left it in, I didn't see Iris. But I did see Toby, crouched by the fire pit and leaning low over it, blowing on a small pile of smoking red pine needles under a tepee of sticks.

"Toby!" I shouted, frantically looking around for the closest source of water.

Toby jumped and spun around, looking equal parts sheepish and triumphant. "It's fine, Dante! I've got it. Promise."

The needles crackled, then gave a pop, scattering in all directions as the wind blew through with a little gust.

"What's going on?" Iris asked, emerging from our tent with a book in hand.

"Water! We need water!" I said gesturing at the fire.

Iris's eyes went wide and she dropped the book, boots grinding on the hard-packed dirt as she spun to run over to River's truck. I went straight for the fire pit, trying to kick dirt on the smoldering needles, not having any luck as my boots scraped against nothing but hard, dry ground. I didn't want to stomp on it and risk sending bits flying out. Toby attempted to shove me back but I wrapped my arms around him and bodily tossed him away from the area, sending him stumbling. He lost his balance and fell backward, arms pinwheeling and landing on his ass.

"Asshole!" Toby said. "That fucking hurt!"

"I'm not the asshole here," I snarled.

Little flames licked up at the tepee of sticks Toby had built over the needles, and they liked what they were tasting. Iris slammed into my side, sticker-covered water bottle in hand, and dumped the contents straight on the fire. It sizzled and spat, the flames gone but wisps of smoke still coming from it. I finally stomped on it for good measure as Iris took up attempting to kick dirt onto everything.

"You two are overreacting!" Toby whined.

"Shut up, Toby!" we both shouted.

"Iris, find more water," I ordered. We had to drown it.

She knelt down at the coolers and started chucking things out in search of liquids as I cast my eyes around for any stray smoldering needles. I was not prepared to hear her yelp, and it snapped my spine straight with fear.

I yanked my head towards her, following her gaze to the edge of the clearing. There was a little trickle of smoke, curling out of a pile of dead aspen leaves from last fall that had collected in the crook between two exposed roots of a half-dead lodgepole pine. Before I could really process what was happening a finger of flame rolled up after the smoke, stretching into the air one inch, two, three.

"Water! More water!" I yelled, running to stomp at the leaves.

I heard Iris and Toby both digging through the coolers behind me now, bits of food smacking into the unforgiving ground. Soon Iris was at my side, pulling me back to make room for a new bottle of water to slosh onto the leaves. Toby stumbled up behind her, arms filled with more bottles and a jug of orange juice. He opened them and handed them off to Iris one by one as I continued to stomp at the persistent flames.

Switching tactics I started using my heel to drag the leaves out, attempting to get it down to bare dirt and starve the flames of fuel. It didn't seem to be working any better, the fire sprawling out in all directions. It was already covering a couple square feet at least. The flames licked at my hiking boot, the heat driving in through the leather, making my foot sweat.

"Dante!" Iris said frantically.

I looked over and saw she was out of liquids. Toby had gone back to the coolers, but he shook his head at me when I looked at him. There was nothing left, even the beer having been sacrificed in an attempt to fight back the flames.

Iris's eyes went somehow wider and without warning she jerked me away from the fire. The flames had grown exponentially in just the moment I'd looked away. Stumbling with Iris, I watched as the flames, backed by another, steadier, gust of wind, raced across the forest floor, gorging on fallen pine needles and scraggly raspberry bushes in a growing arc. When it reached the foot of the lodgepole pine once more the fire seemed stymied for a moment, licking at the bark but not finding purchase. Undeterred it sent out an advance party of embers to float among the branches. One by one the embers alighted, nestling into the crooks of the dead needles and smoldering until, one by one, several crown fires flared to life. The tree became a torch, the flames howling with victory. Their first true victim had been claimed and soon hundreds, thousands, millions more would fall.

Toby just stood there, staring dumbly at the flames as Iris and I darted towards River's truck, only stumbling after us a moment later.

"Call 911! Now!" I gasped, fear making my chest tight. I knew what was coming. Knew it was probably already too late to do anything about it. We had to get out of here.

The heat from the burning tree was already blistering against my back as I dug my phone out so I could just call myself, forcing my hands to stay steady as I dialed. Holding it to my ear, I waited. And waited. There was only silence.

Pulling the phone back around to my face, I checked my bars. None.

"No service!" I said, turning back around to look at the tree.

It almost hurt to look at, the brightest thing on our evening shadowed part of the ridge. The flames were dancing among the long dead branches, elated at how easy it was for them to get hold. The few branches that still had green on them were holding out, but they wouldn't last long.

"I don't have any either," Iris said, voice shaking. Several tears ran down her face, carving tracks through the light coat of dust from driving up with the windows down. "Toby?"

Toby shook his head, mashing down the button on the side of his phone to turn it off and back on. Sometimes you had to do that up here, to get phones to see the towers correctly. Other times the signals just played by mysterious rules that no one understood. All three of us held our breath, but when his home screen came back the top left corner still said "No Service."

I made a split-second decision, the crackling of the tree behind me drilling into my ears. "Iris, Toby, get in the truck and drive until you get a signal. I'm going to find River and Natalie. Make the call and come back for us."

To her credit, and despite her fear, Iris agreed without hesitation.

"We don't have the keys!" Toby said. His eyes kept darting towards the fire, and each time he'd shuffle another step farther away.

"They're on the dashboard," Iris told him, standing on her tiptoes to wrap me in a hug. I squeezed her tight, then let go and watched her climb into the passenger seat.

"I don't want to drive," Toby complained, not moving to get into the truck.. His thumbs were hanging through his belt loops and if it weren't for his constant sideways shuffling, he would have looked like he was enjoying any other day in the woods.

"Well I can't drive stick so fucking suck it up," Iris snapped, slamming the door.

"Now," I ordered when Toby didn't move.

He stared at the tree for a few seconds before finally doing as told, stomping around the hood and sliding into the driver's seat. It took him three tries to get the key into the ignition before the truck roared to life, and he almost slammed the back bumper into an outcropping of rock as he attempted to turn around. Eventually, he got the truck pointed in the right direction and let it loose down the road, back the way we'd come.

Giving the tree one last look—it was fully torching now, the flames beginning to leap to neighboring branches on surrounding trees—I took off in the direction River and Natalie had gone, screaming their names.

CHAPTER 3: CLOCKING IN

Adam

"Oh come on, Delgado, no way you took another night shift!" Shawn called as I hopped out of my pathetic little Honda. Probably a Honda. It was a scrapyard car that had originally been destined for the yearly demolition derby, so, really, it could be anything.

"You know me, always willing to cover," I shouted back, grabbing my lunch bag, hardhat, and safety vest out of the backseat.

"Boy, you're gonna burn yourself out, and you're only eighteen. This'll make, what, fifty-four hours on the clock this week?" our shift supervisor, Elliot, said.

I shrugged, setting my lunch down at my feet to shrug into my vest and hat. A stiff wind was picking up, flapping my vest around until I managed to capture it in the proper orientation to slide my arms through the holes. I pulled my hair back into a stubby ponytail at the nape of my neck first then settled my hardhat on, making sure it was sitting properly.

It wasn't that I liked working at the mine, but I also didn't hate it. The pay was good, the work manageable if strenuous at times, and hours easy to pick up. Better than sitting on my ass at the lake all day, checking the boats of rich tourists for zebra mussels, or fighting with out-of-town hunters at the gas station about the price of chewing tobacco.

"Still saving for your little sister's Girl Scout stuff?" Shawn asked.

I nodded. This was the last shift I needed to afford to send them both to two weeks of summer camp next year. My aunt and uncle had tried to insist they would pay for it, but their finances were strained enough by taking on three kids they'd never intended to have. I loved them for what they'd done for my sisters and me after our parents died, but providing food, shelter, and love was enough. I was determined to take care of the rest myself.

Elliot eyed me, eventually shaking his head without saying anything, turning his attention to the rest of the group. We were all gathered around in the parking lot, waiting for a transport cart into the mine. Thermoses of coffee were glued to most people's hands, many still yawning off a day of sleep.

"Morning, boys," Elliot said. "Workin' the same spot as yesterday. Remember, production was down three-percent last week, so we've gotta keep hitting it hard these last two days of this week. We go down again and someone's ass is on the line."

A mumbled chorus of assent answered him. It'd be another fifteen or so minutes before transport showed up, given that one of the carts was down for maintenance, so everyone scattered around the lot, enjoying the last rays of sunlight. I went back and leaned against my trunk, casting my eyes over the view. A few ridges, ugly with beetle kill, were closest, but behind them the peaks soared up, a few patches of snow still clinging to shaded spots at their tops. Hottest summer on record but those patches were still there. I always found myself checking on them, rooting for them to make it all the way through until new snow came. I kept meaning to look up when something qualified as a glacier, but I still hadn't gotten around to it.

The scent of barbecue came on the wind from the direction of Miner's Village, which was nestled between the first ridge and the second. It made my mouth water. All I'd had for dinner was a couple microwaved breakfast sandwiches that left my mouth feeling tacky.

As I brought my eyes back down from the peaks, a flare of color on the second ridge out caught my attention. I squinted, trying to make out what it could be. Dusk was falling, leaving most of the area in shadow, but I thought I saw...something. Stepping away from my car I went over to the edge of the lot, putting the lot lights behind me so my eyes might adjust better.

There it was again. The faintest flicker of orange. Warm light dancing behind the trees.

"Whatchya looking at?" Shawn called from a bench by the security station at the entrance to the lot.

"You see that glow?" I called back, pointing to the spot. It was maybe half a mile off, at most.

"Eh, probably the setting sun reflecting off some camper's windshield or something," Shawn called back. "That's one of the Lost Hen campgrounds, I think. Always a lot of people up there this time of year. Might even be my kid and his friends, they went up somewhere this morning. Can't remember where."

I frowned, trying to decide if he was right. Could it be just the sun on a windshield? Or maybe the sun on something hung in a tree...a carabiner holding up a bag of food to keep it away from the bears, or one of those portable showers for the city people that couldn't go a weekend without washing off. There was just enough sun left, kissing the tops of the trees, for it to be plausible.

A horn honked behind me, signaling the arrival of a cart ready to load us up and take us to work. After a moment of hesitation I turned away, mind still chewing on what might be on the ridge. The deepest part of my gut was still unsettled for a reason I couldn't pinpoint, but I couldn't afford to get docked for missing the cart and showing up late. Everyone else was already loaded up and I took the last seat at the back, facing Shawn, our knees knocking together in the slim space.

"So, anyone else going to watch the high school charity game next weekend? My boy Dante's play— FUCK!" His words cut off as his eyes went wide, eyebrows shooting high enough to tilt his hardhat back. He was looking over my shoulder at the spot I'd pointed out the strange light.

I spun around, as did everyone else on my half of the cart, and saw that it was no longer a little flickering light. It was a fire. A single tall pine was aflame, fire lashing into the sky above. In the few seconds it took me to realize what was happening several more trees went up, one after the other.

It hadn't rained.
It hadn't rained.
It hadn't rained.
When had it last rained?
Months ago.
It hadn't rained in months.

The sound of pockets being dug into flared out as everyone scrambled from the cart. Someone ran and pounded on the security shed until the guard came out. He took one look at where everyone was pointing and dove back into his shed, leaving the door hanging open. Within a minute half-a-dozen voices were explaining the fire, where it was, how fast it was growing. There weren't enough county dispatchers to take all the calls at once. Some would've re-routed to the state patrol, which was probably good. The more people immediately responding to this the better.

It hadn't rained in months.

I did the math in my head, a mental map laid out. The wind mostly came out of the west this time of year, and it could gust at hurricane forces. Even now it was coming from that direction, pressing lightly against my face as I watched the flames. That meant the fire would likely be pushed east. Except for the mine and Miner's Village, there was twenty miles of forest to the east before anything major was in danger, though there were a few large ranches just to the south east. In a healthy forest that might be enough of a buffer. This wasn't a healthy forest. Not after the logging and poor forestry and pine beetles. Not with the changing climate.

It hadn't rained in months.

Not to mention the mine was the biggest employer in the county. In several counties, in fact. If it went up, the ripple effects would be catastrophic.

It hadn't rained in months.

By now everyone had hung up their phones and gathered at the edge of the lot to watch. At least an acre was already ablaze, the flames scattering across the ridge, jumping from tree to tree. A few guys had pulled binoculars out of their cars and were passing them around. Embers rose into the sky like fireworks, got caught in the wind, and rained back down, starting more fires ahead of the main one.

"What did dispatch say?" I asked Elliot.

He shook his head, a grim look on his face. "Said they were sending an engine out from Sadie's Hill to assess."

"Sadie's Hill?" I said, astounded. Though, really, where else could it have come from? It still just felt wrong. "Elliot, that's forty-five minutes away! And they're going to need a lot more than one damn engine! There isn't a—a chopper with a water bucket or something?"

His eyes swept back and forth, assessing the ridge and the flames. No one knew this land better than him. He was a fifth-generation resident of the area. His family helped found Sadie's Hill. "Not one close enough," he said, voice clipped.

"We have water trucks," I said desperately. "They're full. We know these roads. We drive them way more than the department ever does, and the fire is *right there*."

He didn't answer.

"Elliot, with this wind, by the time they get here that fire will have destroyed half the county."

"My brother's the captain of those firefighters," Elliot said. "He knows the roads."

"And can you guarantee he'll be on whatever engine they send out?" I asked. "We can't just stand here and watch!"

Elliot's jaw clenched. "Adam, I can't order y'all to go out there! You're not firefighters! You'll be in the way! Look how much that damn thing has grown already! You feel that wind? It's going to push this hard."

"That's my point!"

"No. Drop it."

Clenching my fists, I turned back to the trees, knowing I wasn't going to get anywhere. Elliot was right. We weren't professionals. We'd be in the way. Have to get rescued. Waste resources. That knowledge did nothing to chase away the helpless feeling clawing up my throat.

I could hear the fire now, a faint popping off in the distance as it hopped from tree to tree. When I was younger, I'd been fascinated by the way different woods burned in our fireplace at home. Lodgepoles, even fresh green ones, burned quick and hot. When they were dried or beetle-killed they went up almost as fast as paper. Spruce burned quick too, crackling and smelling like Christmas the whole time. Aspen burned slower, especially the bark. There were many nights where an aspen log went on the fire at bedtime and there was still a shell of smoldering bark come morning.

"Answer, answer..." Shawn mumbled.

I looked over at him to see he was stabbing at his phone with his finger. His shoulders were curled forward towards the device, face lit up from the glow of the screen. Pulling it up to his ear, he waited several seconds, then cursed, chucking his hardhat off and sending it skittering across the ground before he hit redial.

"What is it?" I asked.

"Dante," Shawn mumbled, redialing again. "He's out camping with friends. I don't know where but...but I think he might've said Lost Hen. Now he's not answering his phone."

Fear twisted at my heart. I knew Dante. Not well, but I liked him. We'd shared a lot of classes before I dropped out and got my GED a year earlier. He'd always been willing to help me with the assignments my ADHD made more difficult.

"Call your wife, maybe she knows where he went for sure," I suggested.

Shawn gave a nod and shakily navigated to his wife's number instead. "Honey, where did the kids go camping?"

I could barely make out her tinny voice through the speaker, but the blood rushing out of Shawn's face told me exactly what she'd said. They'd gone to Lost Hen.

"Why?" she asked.

Shawn looked at me, eyes desperate. I didn't have an answer for him to give.

"Honey, I'm...I'm in the parking lot at work. There's a fire at Lost Hen. It's growing."

She didn't answer.

"Who was he with?" Shawn asked, voice thick with emotion.

She rattled off a few names that I didn't catch.

"I'm calling the fire department back, I'll call you as soon as I know anything," Shawn said.

As he called the fire department, I turned to look at our three tender trucks. Dented and dinged, paint peeling and chrome faded, all three were retired fire engines bought at auction by the mine, each older than I was. We used them to spray down the dirt roads around the mine and settling ponds, more to cut down on the dust than anything, but there was no reason they couldn't still fight fires. They had all their hoses and, though the sirens had been disabled, the horns were atrociously loud. Two of them held 1,800 gallons, the other held 1,500. All would have been filled by the day shift at the end of their day, ready for the next day shift tomorrow. All had radios that would work at least somewhat better than cellphones once we left the range of the mine's cell signal boosters.

I'd never driven them myself, but I knew the keys were in the security shed. I'd seen our road crew check them out dozens of times.

Glancing around, I found the guard standing in a small cluster of people with Elliot, all with their backs to the lot as they watched the fire through binoculars. It had to be at least twenty acres already. Keeping my eyes on them, I slipped closer to the shed. One last check that their attention was occupied, and I ducked inside.

A single bare bulb lit the closet-sized space. There was only enough room for a desk, a computer monitor displaying a grid of camera feeds, and not much else. The keys were on a pegboard on the wall opposite the door. Scanning my eyes down them, I found the sets for the tenders, taking the keys for the two biggest.

No one noticed me coming back out of the shed. They were too distracted by the ash that had begun to drift down, larger chunks pattering against the ground, sounding exactly like rain.

Shawn was standing where I left him, hands on the back of his head, fingers tangled in his box braids. I stepped in front of him and when he dropped his hands I pressed a set of keys into one, tilting my head in the direction of the tankers.

"Let's go," I said.

He took a quick glance at the keys I'd given him, another at the fire, and nodded once. "But you're staying."

"I'm just going to agree to get you to go and then take my own," I said, flashing the second set of keys. "So let's not waste time arguing."

"Adam, not only is this stupid dangerous, you'll get arrested for stealing the truck," Shawn hissed. "You think they'll listen to a Mexican dropout about his good intentions? I doubt they'll treat a Black man like me any better, but it's my son out there."

I swallowed once, mind flashing to my sisters. There were only a few cops in our town, and I knew all of them somewhat—hard not to in a town our size—but they were still cops. White cops. Then there were the stateys, and I didn't know any of them. Not to mention what the company might do to me even *if* the cops didn't do anything.

"Maybe I will," I admitted. "But I'll take a few years or whatever in jail over letting people die. It might not just be Dante and his friends. There's five campgrounds up there, plus trails and the Village."

Shawn glanced at the fire once again, swallowed heavily, then turned his eyes back to me and nodded. "Let's go. I'll take Gulch Road, you take County Road 32, circle up from there. We should meet back up near the top of Lost Hen. Radio if you find anyone."

I nodded.

"Stop at the Village too. They probably can't see how bad the fire is yet. Tell them to get out," Shawn suggested.

I nodded again, clutching my keys tightly.

A few of the guys glanced at us as Shawn and I made our way to the trucks, but Elliot's attention was firmly on the fire. He was back on the phone with someone. I was far enough away now that I couldn't make out his words.

The handle of the driver's side door was at my eye level, a corrugated metal step providing access to the raised cab. I unlocked it quick but opened the door slow, knowing it was going to screech if I went too fast. Climbing up I settled onto the faded, tattered gray bench seat that stretched from door to door. Aside from layers of dirt, the cab was relatively clean. Signs of age were everywhere, though. The radio wasn't original, gaps around its sides, and someone had replaced the gearshift knob with an 8-ball. The dashboard was scratched to hell and stuffing poofed out of several holes in the seat. I didn't need pretty, though. I needed functional.

Glancing over at Shawn in the next truck over I gave him a nod that he returned. He held up three fingers, putting them down one by one. When the last one dropped, we both twisted our keys and slammed the clutches before throwing the trucks into motion, grateful they'd been pointed forward so we didn't have to turn around. There was no missing the sound of these trucks roaring to life, and everyone in the lot turned to look. Elliot's jaw dropped. By the time he started running for the trucks, Shawn and I were already halfway to the gate. I heard Elliot's hand slam against my passenger door, his head barely visible over the bottom of the window. It sounded like he was yelling, but I couldn't make out the words over the sound of the engine.

The gate was down and Shawn rammed through the thin strip of plywood without hesitation. I followed, feeling my tires bump over the wood as I turned up the volume on the CB radio, hoping to hear something from the firefighters, thought I wasn't even sure if it was the right kind of radio for that. Shawn split off from me halfway down the hill the mine sat on, turning onto Gulch Road. I couldn't see him, and I knew he couldn't see me, but I gave him a little wave nonetheless as I carried on down to the highway, heading for the Village.

Troublesome Dispatch: All units be advised, there has been a report of a possible wildfire in the Lost Hen campground area. Flames have been sighted. Unit 41 in route to assess.

Captain Henderson: Who is our reporting party?

Troublesome Dispatch: We've received multiple calls from your brother and others up at the mine. They can see flames from their parking lot, about half a mile due west of them.

Captain Henderson: Do we know the status of any campers in that area right now?

Troublesome Dispatch: No, sir.

Captain Henderson: What's 41's ETA?

Troublesome Dispatch: Forty-five minutes.

Captain Henderson: We got anyone closer?

Troublesome Dispatch: No, sir.

Captain Henderson: Air support?

Troublesome Dispatch: Working on it. Most resources are already at the Elk Canyon fire three counties down. They lost most of their lines today. Our request for air support has been made and will be honored as soon as possible, but they're still figuring out what they can send.

Captain Henderson: Understood.

Troublesome Dispatch: All units be advised, we received another call from someone at the mine. He believes his seventeen-year-old son and four other teenagers may be camping in the area. He has attempted to contact his son without—

Captain Henderson: Susan? You cut out there.

Troublesome Dispatch: Hang on.

Troublesome Dispatch: Your brother just called again. Two of the miners have stolen two of the mine's water trucks and headed for the fire. One of them is the father of the kid who is out camping with friends.

Captain Henderson: …

Troublesome Dispatch: Do you copy?

Captain Henderson: I copy. What's 41s ETA? And who else has gone out?

Troublesome Dispatch: Forty minutes for 41. 46 and 48 are on their way now as well, ETA forty-five minutes for both. 50 is on another call for an animal vs. vehicle incident with minor injuries. Other resources are coming in from farther, but their ETAs are unknown at this time.

Captain Henderson: …Godspeed to those miners. Get me descriptions of the trucks they're in and of them. And find out if their trucks have working radios, and what kinds.

CHAPTER 4: THE GLOW

River

Dusty wind scraped at my exposed skin, but I was too distracted to care. The only sensations that mattered were Natalie's fingers grazing lightly along my sides, sending shivers up my spine, and her lips melding to mine. I didn't even care that our hair kept getting tangled around our heads; there wasn't room for it to get in the way of kissing, so it didn't matter.

We had to catch our breath eventually though, pulling apart to grin deliriously at one another.

"Hi," I said.

"Hi," she echoed.

A look of distraction fell over Natalie's face and she bit her lip, glancing back in the direction we'd come. "Do you think he'll ever grow up?"

I sighed. "I think I don't feel like talking about Toby while I'm kissing my way down your neck," I replied. She was sitting on a waist-high stump, giving me plenty of access as I leaned back in to kiss along her jaw.

She gave a little gasp, tilting her head back. "Fair."

I continued my path down the column of her throat, stopping to pay special attention to the spots where her shoulder blades met her collarbones, knowing they were some of her favorites, kissing my way between them along her collarbones. Her shirt was long gone, as was mine, tossed off into the dirt somewhere, and, though I didn't remember doing it, her lavender bra straps had been slid out of the way.

"It's just..." she trailed off.

I groaned and pulled away. "Babe. Please."

"I'm sorry, I'm sorry, he's just. Ugh. I know he can be...a lot. But I've lived across the street from him my whole life! He's like the brother I never wanted and can't get rid of but also can't stop loving. I've spent so many sleepovers at his house, and so many afternoons helping him and his mom with her cupcake business when orders got backed up, and he always protected me from bullies when we were little. But the last couple years...it's like all those nice parts of him are trickling away one by one."

I sighed, bracketing my hands around her hips and thunking our foreheads together lightly. "I'm not sure what you want me to say here."

"Tell me if you think he'll grow up, grow out of this stupid phase he's in," Natalie said. There was real concern in her deep brown eyes, and I would've given anything to chase it away.

"Not anytime soon," I said, cupping her face and running my thumb along her cheek. "Sorry. But if totaling his jeep didn't do it, I don't know what will."

She sniffed, leaning into my hand. "I know it's terrible, but I kind of...wish he'd gotten hurt in that crash? Not bad or anything! Just. A broken arm or concussion. Something other than walking away from it without a scratch. Maybe that would've been enough."

"Even that may not have done it," I said gently. "He would've been thrilled to get a scar and a cool story."

I pulled her into a hug as her eyes sparkled with tears, wrapping my arms tight around her. She returned the gesture, clasping onto me with her head tucked against my shoulder. Her skin felt so warm against mine. Soft everywhere but her hands, which were calloused from constant work outside. Stroking my fingers lightly up and down her spine, I turned and kissed her hair. It smelled like peaches from her morning shower.

After a moment she pulled back, letting out a watery laugh as she swiped at her eyes. "Sorry for ruining the makeout session."

"Eh, we'll have plenty more."

Damn she was pretty. The last bits of the golden hour lit her up, throwing everything I loved into contrast and dipping it in honey. Once again, I reached my hand up and brushed the pad of my thumb across one of her cheeks, thinking I needed to count her freckles before summer ended and they faded. Maybe I'd start keeping track. See how different they were year by year.

She let her head fall to the side, nuzzling into my hand and an involuntary sound escaped my lips. A lopsided grin wound its way across her face as she looked up at me through her eyelashes, knowing exactly what she was doing to me.

"You are the best kind of torture," I breathed, leaning back in for a messy kiss.

She giggled against my lips, throwing her legs around my hips to pull me in closer.

It wasn't long before I was making my way back down her neck, intending to make it much lower this time.

Until she screamed.

A lot of thoughts raced through my mind, more concepts than tangible ideas, and chief among them was a cougar. She wouldn't scream over a bear. She wouldn't scream over a moose. She probably wouldn't even scream over a nut with a gun. What else was there?

"What? What?" I said, scrambling upright and spinning around.

In front of me was the path back to the campsite. Fifty yards up a ridge, a bit of a clamber over a dirt bank, and then another fifty yards to our friends. It was all mostly sage and a few stumps, with the lodgepoles not starting until the top of the bank. A warm, orange glow emanated from behind the trees. For a moment I thought it was the sunset. Except it was coming from the wrong direction.

"Oh my god, oh my god, oh my god!" Natalie said, hands gripping onto my left arm so tight my fingers started to tingle.

"DANTE! IRIS! TOBY!" I screamed, wind snatching at the words.

No answer came.

"DANTE! IRIS! TOBY!" We screamed together.

No answer came, except for the first flames joining the glow. They didn't come from the ground but from the sky. An ember blew towards us, catching in the needles halfway up a lodgepole.

I couldn't tell if I heard the pop as the needles burst into flame, or imagined it. It didn't matter.

"River!" Natalie said, voice shaking.

We had our phones, not that it mattered. There wouldn't be signal out here. There was a mountain in the way of us and the closest tower, and the signal booster they used at the mine didn't have enough range to help us all the way out here.

The heat from the fire was becoming apparent, soaking into my face like a summer day that was on the edge of unbearable.

"There's no way back," I realized.

Natalie keened softly, starting to shake.

I spun around, desperately taking in the terrain, searching for a path. We were in the bottom of a shallow bowl on the hillside, the wind bringing the fire right on top of us. The only accessible path back to the campsite, to our friends, to my truck, to a way out, was through the fire. Once the fire crested the draw it was now working its way up, it would slow somewhat burning downhill towards us. But it wasn't much of a hill, and it was patchworked with forest. Any attempt to make for the top of the ridge would be cut off before we could get there.

"We have to go," I said, desperately searching around until I found our shirts caught in a couple bushes. Natalie took hers and we both yanked them on. Grabbing her hand, I tugged her down the slope.

"There's nothing that way, River! Just the mine. It's twen—twenty miles to the next town! There's nothing but wilderness," she stuttered.

"We don't have another way out! We have to run, Natalie, now! We'll find the road and go around and out the bottom!" I shouted, unable to control the volume of my voice.

Another small, scared noise escaped her, but she nodded, clasping my hand tightly.

The fire at our backs was howling now. I spared it one last glance, squeezed Natalie's hand, and started to run.

When I was a kid, I ran through the forest like nothing

mattered. Fallen trees were things to spring off of, sage bushes objects to weave and dodge, woodchuck holes something to jump. So what if I tripped? I could roll and keep on going.

I hadn't run like that in years, and I couldn't make my brain remember how to do it now that everything mattered. The logs were insurmountable; how had I ever jumped them? The sage was thick and wild, grabbing at my clothes and pulling me back; how had I ever dodged it? The woodchuck holes appeared out of nowhere, attempting to swallow my feet and break my ankles; where did my ability to spot them go?

The fire was following us downhill, sticking mostly to the trees but spreading out among the sage as well. It was slower than us, for now, but the wind was pushing it ever closer.

"Where are we going?" Natalie gasped out. We'd quickly given up on holding hands, both of us unable to run effectively that way.

"We need to find the road," I said, stringing the plan together as I spoke. "It switchbacks up this part of the ridge, we have to cross it somewhere if we go this way."

"Somewhere?" Natalie tripped and I caught her, hauling her back to her feet. The slope was getting steeper, forcing us to stumble sideways more than run. There wasn't time to go along the contour of the hillside until we found a better way down.

"I'll know it when I see it," I promised, hoping it wasn't a lie.

I pushed Natalie ahead so I could keep an eye on her. If I was wrong about the road, if I couldn't find it, the fire was going to catch us. How long had we been running? Seconds? Minutes? Where were Dante, Iris, and Toby?

I took a risk, aware it might make me fall, and glanced back at the flames. They were maybe a-hundred-and-fifty yards behind us and to our right, but we were running out of sage and would soon be back in the trees. Back in the heavy fuels. You didn't grow up in the mountains without learning about fire; basic survival lessons were part of gym class. But no amount of recitation about fuel types and wind directions and escaping an aspen grove full of fake smoke mattered now.

Except....

I thought about the three little matches in my pocket. Ever since I was little my father had made sure I knew to leave the house with at least three matches and a pocketknife. "You never know when you'll get stuck somewhere, baby girl, and a few matches will keep you warm until someone can find you."

We'd watched a lot of educational videos about wildfires in gym class, one mentioning the concept of escape fires. The idea was that you found an open area, burned it down ahead of the main fire, then laid down in the ashes as the main fire passed over. Theoretically, it would pass you by as there was nothing left around you to burn. You might get cooked by radiant heat, or suffocated by smoke, but at least you wouldn't burn directly.

Sage as tall as my waist wasn't exactly an open area, though. I doubted that I could get it to burn fast enough to really build an escape area. Deciding against it, I took off after Natalie once more. We'd just have to hope we made it back out of the trees before the fire caught up.

CHAPTER 5: CALL FOR HELP

Iris

"I don't see what the big deal is," Toby muttered. His hand on the gearshift kept clutching and unclutching around the knob.

I ignored him, holding both our phones up and swinging them around the cab in a desperate search for signal. The little "No Service" indicator remained firmly in place on both phones.

Toby screwed up a shift and the truck made an alarming noise which only made him swear and complain that just because he knew how to drive stick didn't mean he knew how to drive River's "ancient piece of shit." I was about ready to punt him out and figure out how to drive myself, lack of experience driving stick be dammed, when he took a turn too fast. The vibrations of the dirt road stopped as the tires lost grip, the truck spinning sideways. Somehow I wasn't even shocked, the only thought going through my brain being, "Of course, why shouldn't this happen too?"

When the truck shuddered to a stop it was tilted slightly sideways, and facing the wrong way, but otherwise, things seemed okay. We were just in a shallow ditch. Nothing steep. Nothing dangerous now that we'd stopped. Nothing we couldn't get out of. Toby was in the driver's seat, eyes wide and hands hovering above the steering wheel.

"We're fine, just go, just go," I told him.

He didn't go.

"Toby!" I shouted, reaching over to grab his arm and shake him.

He took several big gulps of air, restarted the truck, then shifted back into gear and pulled us out of the ditch, starting a three-point turn. It was quickly apparent, however, that we were not as fine as I had assumed. A strange flopping, dragging sound was coming from behind me and the truck was not sitting level on the roadway. I had the door open before Toby even fully stopped, hanging onto the Oh Shit handle as I leaned out to look at the back passenger tire. It was popped, a huge puncture down one side.

"Fuck all!" I shouted, getting out once the truck stopped moving. I dropped to the ground, peering underneath the bed, fear building in my stomach as I looked for the spare tire. It was there. Caked in mud, but there.

Toby came around to stand next to me, hands fisted and pressed into the back of his head.

I scrambled back to my feet, grabbing the phones out of the cab. They both still said no signal.

"Toby, I'm going to run for it," I told him. "Change the tire and catch up with me when you can."

"I don't know how to change a tire!" Toby whined.

My jaw dropped open. "What?"

"I have Triple A!'"

"Well, they sure as hell ain't comin' out here!" I snapped.

Toby looked at me like I'd kicked him, all wide blue eyes and confused eyebrows. In that moment I couldn't stand him, couldn't stand that he'd probably never been yelled at in his life, never suffered a consequence, never been held responsible for anything. Everything in me wanted to scream at him, to call him every name in the book, plus a few of the ones our French teacher had secretly taught us.

"Grow the fuck up!" I finally shouted. "You did this, Toby! All of this! Stop whining and moaning and deal with it!" Leaning into the cab and across the seat, I pulled the keys out of the ignition, then climbed into the bed of the truck to unlock River's truckbox. "Look in the glove compartment for the manual," I told Toby. "It should have instructions."

"Can't you do it?" Toby whined.

"No! I have to go find a damn signal!" I told him, digging through River's mess of tools and camping equipment in search of a jack.

"I'll run and find signal," Toby tried. "I'll come back for you to drive the truck, I promise!"

I glared down at him. "I don't trust you. Not to make the call, or to come back."

He huffed and rolled his eyes, slumping towards the cab and opening the glovebox, all the while grumbling under his breath about how none of this was his fault so I shouldn't be yelling at him.

If we didn't get this taken care of quick we might be better off abandoning the truck entirely, but a big part of me doubted that Toby would make it out if we did. The extent of his physical fitness was playing VR boxing games. As much as he annoyed me, I wasn't going to leave him behind to burn.

"Found it," Toby declared, holding up the tattered manual.

"Look up the tire change section," I instructed when he didn't do anything else. This idiot was never going to be able to function in the real world. Not that it mattered, as he'd never be a part of it with money like his.

I found the jack nestled under a crumpled tarp and pulled it out, revealing a flash of red underneath. At first my mind refused to parse what I was seeing. Had it really been there the whole time? Why the hell hadn't I looked in here? Of course someone as prepared as River would have one in her truck.

I hopped down from the bed, shoving the jack towards Toby, along with the fire extinguisher.

"This could've put it out!" he said, tone aghast like it was my fault we hadn't known the thing existed.

"And you could've kept it from starting in the first place," I retorted, picking both phones up once more. "Change the damn tire."

With that I took off, pelting down the road.

Leg strength was an important aspect of horse riding, but lately most of my exercise focused on core strength. It took a lot to stay upright in the saddle when your horse was twisting sideways around a barrel. My legs were burning before I knew it, knees sparking with agony as my feet slammed down onto the hard packed dirt that sloped down in front of me.

There was little sun left now, just ambient evening light and a warm wind. The air didn't seem to be cooling with the loss of the sun, or maybe that was my adrenaline lying to me.

When I came to the next bend in the road, I stopped to catch my breath and check the phones. Still no signal. I cursed and looked back, trying to see the fire, but the view was obscured by trees. All I could make out was a billow of smoke, pluming out into the sky in great, roiling torrents painted orange at the top by the last bits of sun that could still reach it. Lower down it was blue-black, except at the very bottom where it glowed ominously. Other people had to have reported it by now, someone at the mine or at the Village, but they wouldn't know that Dante, River, and Natalie were stuck out there. Maybe the kids in the Village would remember us going by, maybe they wouldn't. Either way, I wasn't willing to put the lives of my friends in the hands of a bunch of random children no older than ten. I had to keep running, find a place to make a call.

Taking off again I made it only twenty yards before my foot caught in a divot and I went sailing forward. Years of riding had me rolling with the impact, letting my shoulder take the brunt of it and spinning the rest away until I found myself sprawled on my back. The sky above me was a deep navy, one or two planets visible ahead of the stars that weren't bright enough to cut through the last bits of daylight.

Scrambling up into a sitting position I looked around for the phones. I found Toby's first, or what was left of it. The screen was shattered and the whole thing bent slightly. Frantically, I swung my eyes around until I saw mine nestled in a tuft of grass off the side of the road. Scooping it up I found the screen with one big crack across the center, yet somehow still glowing with life.

And it had one bar.

I mashed in 911, fingers shaking, and held my breath.

"Troublesome County 911, do you need fire, police, or EMS?" A woman's steady, kind voice said.

"Fire," I gasped, kneading a stitch in my side with a couple curled knuckles.

"Is this about the Lost Hen fire or another fire?"

They knew. Thank god.

"Lost Hen," I said. "My friends and I were out camping where the fire started." It was taking a lot of effort to get my words out as I continued to struggle to catch my breath. "We didn't have signal, two of my friends were away from camp, another friend went to find them, and then Toby and I went to drive and get signal."

"Slow down, honey. Your friends are stuck near the fire?"

"Yes." I decided to sit down, hoping it would help.

"How many people?"

"Three."

"How old are they? What are they wearing?"

I gave the dispatcher all the details, telling her about Dante's blue flannel, River's sage green t-shirt, and Natalie's red 4H t-shirt.

"Okay, honey, we've already got several engines on the way. You said you and another friend were heading down the mountain?"

"We're trying," I said, finally able to breathe a bit. "He popped a tire on the truck, I left him behind to change it while I ran to get a signal. He hasn't caught up."

"Is the fire close to you?"

I couldn't tell. The smoke plume was getting bigger, the bottom glowing brighter. "I don't know."

"Okay, honey, I'm going to need you to keep going down the mountain. I've passed the last known location of all your friends to our crews and they'll be there as soon as they can."

I frowned. "As soon as they can?"

The line was silent.

"What do you mean 'as soon as they can'? How far away are they?"

"Honey, I need you to get going."

"How far?" I demanded, getting back to my feet.

"Please get going, the less people our officers and firefighters have to worry about, the easier it will be for th—"

"Fuck you!" I cut in. "I'm going back for my friends."

Her unwillingness to answer was answer enough. No one was getting here anytime soon. No one ever did in the mountains. You didn't live out here without knowing that it meant you were usually on your own, no matter how bad things got. Hanging up the phone I turned to head back up the road, back to Toby. If he didn't have the tire changed by the time I got there...well I didn't know what I'd do, but he wasn't going to like it.

The worry proved to be unfounded within minutes when River's truck came rolling down the road, skidding to a stop next to me. A quick glance at the back showed that the spare tire at least seemed to be on correctly. Hopefully he'd tightened the lugnuts enough. I clambered into the cab, finding the fire extinguisher in the passenger footwell.

"Did you get signal?" Toby asked.

"Yeah. The fire's been reported but no one is getting here soon enough," I fumed. I wasn't even sure who I was the maddest at at this point. Toby. Dispatch. Our fire department. Long dead loggers with bad forestry practices. Companies destroying the climate. So many options. "Turn us around, we've got to pick up the others."

"But the fire," Toby moaned.

I spun in my seat and slapped him across the face, not bothering to check the force. "Our friends are up there! Turn around now!"

He recoiled, pressing his back against the driver's side door and looking at me with wide eyes.

"Iris—"

"Go get them!" I shouted, tears leaking out of my eyes. "They need us! They don't have a way out and help won't get here in time! Stop being a coward!"

Still he didn't move.

I growled in frustration and threw myself out of the truck, going around to the other side and pulling the door open. Toby nearly fell out and I shoved him back in, reaching over his lap to unbuckle the seatbelt. I kept shoving him until he got the message and clambered over the center console into the passenger seat. I slid into his place and took a deep breath, trying to steady myself.

My parents had both tried to teach me to drive stick and, technically, I knew all the right steps to make it work. I just also found it incredibly distracting to try and remember all of them while actually driving, which had resulted in several unintended off-roading adventures while learning. I'd accepted a life of driving automatics at this point and hadn't practiced stick in months. But River, Natalie, and Dante needed me to get them out.

Taking one more deep breath I eased the truck into reverse, putting the back wheels into the shallow ditch so I'd have room to turn around, then shifted it into first and headed back up the mountain.

Troublesome Dispatch: All units be advised, we have tentative locations on the five missing teenagers. They were camped at campground four and two of them, River Ashworth and Natalie McLain, split off to the north prior to the fire. Two, Toby Cassidy and Iris Sawyer, left camp after the fire started and headed down Dirty Bird road to get cell signal. The fifth, Dante Kristofferson, went to find River and Natalie. Toby and Iris may have gone back up the mountain to retrieve their friends after making their call. 41s ETA is thirty minutes. Six more engines have been dispatched from local departments as well.

Captain Henderson: Did you say Dante's out there? Our volunteer Dante?

Troublesome Dispatch: Unfortunately yes. But maybe that's good? The kid may not officially be on your crew, but he's been shadowing you for years now. He knows what to do.

Captain Henderson: I hope you're right. What's the status of air support?

Troublesome Dispatch: A type two helicopter with night flight certification has been dispatched from the Elk Canyon fire to assess, but it had to refuel first. Its ETA is one hour, depending on wind conditions.

Captain Henderson: What else?

Troublesome Dispatch: That's it for now. They're the only available crew with night certification, everything else is grounded until dawn.

Captain Henderson: Tell them there are people trapped out there! Elk Canyon is only burning wilderness, we have people in danger. Lives come before structures come before forests.

Elliot: This is Elliot Henderson from the Molly Mine, anyone copy?

Captain Henderson: We copy, Elliot.

Elliot: A copter won't get those kids out, Jake, you know that. There's nowhere for one to land. Even if it can find them and do a damn water drop on their heads, it wouldn't be enough. Those kids' best hope is my guys in the trucks, and yours if they can make it in time.

Captain Henderson: We should be better than this. I'm on my way in a type six with a few more guys who were off duty. Keep me updated on your guys, Elliot.

CHAPTER 6: RUNNING

River

My calves felt like they were burning as badly as the forest. We were back in the trees now, though they were sparse for the moment. Ash coated my tongue, smoke slithered down my throat, rolling around in my lungs, and sparks settled in my hair as it whipped behind me. Could I tell if I caught fire? Or would it feel the same as the heat from the torching trees around me?

Flashes of Natalie in my peripheral were all that kept me going. If I gave up she'd give up, which wasn't an option. We hadn't tried to speak since we started running again. Occasional bumps of our pumping arms were the only comfort we had.

The terrain was becoming steeper and steeper as we went, forcing us into an awkward jumping, loping gait. Powder dry dirt gave way with every step we took, forcing us into the next and the next and the next without time to think between each. What scraggly plants grew on the slope weren't tall enough or frequent enough to provide any hand holds, leaving us with only luck to keep us upright. The plants were all more than enough to burn, though, so there was no safety to be found.

The fire was a complete unknown now. Behind us, yes. But how far? I couldn't risk turning to find out. The heat was enough to say it was too close.

Where was the damn road? Had we missed it, or not reached it yet? If we could just cross a switchback we'd have a way out. The road would be a firebreak, and a much easier surface to sprint across, but it remained elusive.

The ground dropped out from under me without warning,

my arms pinwheeling to keep me upright. It wasn't enough, though, my body pitching forward into a roll. Some distant part of my brain remembered enough childhood gymnastic lessons for me to take the impact without injury, one hand managing to snag a handful of grass and arrest my momentum after several tumbles. When I got my bearings I realized Natalie had skidded to a stop a few feet down the hill from me when she saw me fall and was watching me with wide eyes. She was already trying to pick her way back to me, grabbing at anything she could for purchase.

"Go, go! I'm okay!" I shouted, digging my heels into the dirt to get back up and going. As I stood I caught a flash of flames off to my right, dancing among a stand of trees. It chewed through them like paper, the roar of its hunger growing louder and louder as it approached.

"River!"

It was so much faster than us.

"RIVER!" A clod of dirt smacked into my thigh.

I jolted, realizing I hadn't started running yet. Natalie had made it a few more feet before noticing I wasn't with her, turning back once more. She didn't start running again before seeing that I had as well.

There was no missing the flames now, no blissful ignorance about how far behind us they may or may not be, because they were right there.

I wanted to go home. I wanted my bed and my goats and my cat. I wanted my mother to come in and kiss me goodnight, which she hadn't done in years. I wanted to make Natalie laugh. I wanted to kick Toby's ass because this had to have been him. Dante was way too educated about fire risk to have started it, and Iris was smart enough to never light a fire on a day like today. Toby, though. Toby was so self-centered that he thought rules didn't apply to him and rich enough that he was usually right.

A flash of blue stopped me short. Blue was the last color I expected to see out here in the desert dry forest among the blazing oranges and yellows that were consuming everything.

Slowing without stopping, I tried to peer through the flames and catch sight of it again, something in my mind insisting this was important.

There it was again. A splash of pale blue about six feet off the ground, thin black and white lines crisscrossing it. I knew that pattern.

"DANTE!" I screamed, freezing where I stood.

Natalie stumbled to a stop as well, twisting her head back and forth. "Where?" she shouted.

"He was there, I know he was there!" I said, even though the flames had concealed him once more.

Natalie struggled back to me, grasping my hand so I could pull her up. A tree fell, sending out a whoosh of wind that pushed away the flames for a moment, revealing Dante again. He seemed to be alone and the sight settled like a rock in my gut. Where were Iris and Toby? Had they been separated from Dante somehow? Dante never would've willingly left Iris behind.

"Can we get through?" Natalie asked, hand still clinging to mine to keep stable.

I shoved my blowing hair out of my face, scanning the line of fire. Dante wasn't all that far away, yet still too far. There was no break.

Dante was screaming something, but the achingly loud noise of the flames stole the sound away. His gestures got the point across anyway, though, frantically waving us down.

"He's so close," Natalie whimpered as I pulled us away.

"Not close enough."

Was this how he'd gotten separated from Iris and Toby? One inconvenient wedge of fire coming between them and forcing them apart bit by bit?

Logic said to put distance between us and the fire, to angle away from it. Desperation said to keep trying to find a way through. Three people were better than two and, since we hadn't hit the road yet, that meant the most likely direction to find it would be towards Dante. Not to mention, if this bit of fire spread out, came in front of us, we'd be done for. Surrounded. Even as I felt the skin of my right arm begin to blister I struggled to pull away. I wanted out. I wanted out. I wanted out.

When a gunshot rang out, audible even over the fire, I had the ridiculous and out-of-place thought that I didn't have any hunter's orange on. Wouldn't that be stupid, dying from an ill-placed shot while running from a wildfire? Who was even shooting, anyway? The first rifle season was weeks away.

A second shot told me the truth of what was happening, though. Flames had reached some greener trees unaffected by the beetles, but with the fire still fueled by all the deadfall scattered across the ground, the green trees didn't stand a chance against the onslaught. Tendrils of flame curled around them, wrapping the trunks in deadly heat until they exploded, the sap inside boiling and expanding so fast it sent slivers of wood rocketing out in all directions. Pop. Pop. Pop. They went faster and faster, like a hellish form of popcorn.

We had no choice but to get farther away now, a decision I made a second too late. A huge Douglas fir in front of us burst, Natalie yelping and my eyes catching a flash of flying debris before I was on the ground and unaware of how I got there. Something was wrong. I knew something was wrong, I just couldn't figure it out. It was dark. Why the hell was it dark?

"River?! River, come on!" Natalie's voice. It was probably her yanking on my arm.

Sensation started to creep back in. Something was wrong.

Part of my face felt like...nothing. It was like someone had turned off the nerves around my eyes and across my forehead. The skin around the nothing was starting to scream.

"River!" Natalie shouted. "We have to go! Get up!"

"I can't see," I said, numbly.

I felt like I was at the bottom of a deep well, everything dulled out. The noise of the fire faded to a distant rumble. The heat searing my skin along my right side became more of a kiss than a bite. The smoke that scraped at my nose and mouth lost its acidic singe. It was all so much less immediate than it had been moments earlier.

I couldn't see. There was a hole in my face and I couldn't see.

Fingers grabbed my chin and tilted my head up, turning

it side to side. Natalie said something I didn't catch, then one of her arms slid under mine, draping my own arm across her shoulders as her other arm went around my waist. She hauled me up, adjusting the pressure around my waist to steer us.

We were going to die now.

We were too slow together, and I wasn't dumb enough to think I could convince her to leave me.

I wanted to go home. I wanted my bed and my goats and my cat. I wanted my mother to come in and kiss me goodnight, which she hadn't done in years. I wanted to make Natalie laugh. I wanted to kick Toby's ass because I knew this had to have been him.

I wanted to see Natalie's face again. I wanted to see the stars. I wanted to see a volcano erupt. I wanted to see a tiger in the wild.

I wanted to go home.

Keeping my feet under me was nearly impossible, my toes catching on everything and my ankles twisting when the ground wasn't where I was expecting. Natalie hauled me up over and over. I didn't know where she was finding the strength. Step by step the dirt came quicker until the ground was flat. Even with the terrain evened out I couldn't make my lower half function the way I wanted.

"A trail!" Natalie gasped. Her chest was heaving against my side, the smoke and exertion pushing her to her limit. "A trail sign!"

"What does it say?" I managed, proud of myself for forming words instead of screams. Whatever was going on with my face was starting to feel like a strange mix of electricity and pins being stabbed into my skin over and over.

"I don't—I don't know," she coughed. "It's old and faded and the letters keep flipping."

Fuck. Between her dyslexia and the stress, there was no way she was going to be able to read the sign in time.

"Where's the fire?" I asked, feeling her twist around to look back. "What directions does the trail go?"

"The fire's a couple hundred yards behind us, and maybe fifty yards to the right. The trail goes down and to the left on one branch, up and to the left on another, and down to the right on another." Her voice was shaky, the shuddering of anxiety indistinguishable from her trembling exertion.

"*Think*," I screamed at myself in my head. I'd been camping up here my whole life. I had to know what trails these were, where they went.

Shrugging Natalie's arm off my shoulders I pushed her forward in the direction I assumed the sign was. Her fingers clung to my shirt but I pushed her again.

"Use your hands to cover the letters, just read me the first one of each line," I said.

She pulled me with her, but then her hands were gone, my throat closing with fear. I knew she hadn't left, that she was still within reach. Still, the terrifying reality of not being able to see hit me all over again when we lost contact. Flailing out I batted around in the air until I caught hold of her shirt, scrunching it in my hands.

"Duh—D," Natalie stuttered out. "Ya—U. Ee—L. A—A—R."

I did know this sign. Dirty Bird, 0.2 miles to our right. Upper Pond 0.25 miles down and to our left. The ridge top two miles up and to the left. We'd missed the road, and the fire would cut us off on that side before we could get to it.

"Down and to the left," I said. "It goes to the pond!"

One of her arms wrapped around my waist again, pulling me left.

The pond was our only chance now. We couldn't run much longer, but if we made it there the water might save us. If the little pond wasn't dry.

CHAPTER 7: SEARCHING

Dante

Before I'd even had a chance to find River and Natalie, the fire had cut me off from the direction they'd gone. My only choice had been to run down the hill, screaming their names as the fire followed. It was burning just as intently on the ground as in the crowns of the trees, fully consuming the forest. When I did find River and Natalie, a finger of flames was still between us. For a moment I'd thought I could get below it and over to them, but before I could a spot fire had started in the direction I'd intended to go. The ground fire arced around ahead of me, cutting me off from them completely. Below me, though, the fire was mostly in the crowns, not on the ground. Maybe I could still make it to them. Knowing it was a risk, knowing it was dumb, knowing it was the wrong decision, I dashed through, under the gathering flames, coming out in an area that was, so far, filled with just smoke.

But I was just as cut off as before, and not by anything I could run through now.

"Shit!" I screamed. This fire was moving so, so fast. Faster than I could plan, faster than I could think.

There was nothing left to do but keep going forward, hoping I'd find some breach in the flames that gave me a way through to River and Natalie.

So I ran, and the only way I could go was back into the worst of the dying forest.

Playing football had nothing on fighting my way through the deadly tumble of fallen trees, heat pressing into my back and smoke snaking into my lungs. Bark bit into my palms as I vaulted some trees and slid under others. I was distantly aware my hands were cut and bleeding, but the pain didn't register in a way I was used to. I knew it was there, knew the injury had happened, was happening, but the actual sensation of it was absent.

The tangle of fallen, jackstrawed pines reared up without warning, now layered so deep the topmost logs were over my head. It was just as bad to my left and right, surrounding me in a wall of uncrossable terrain. It made the earlier stretch with a single layer of fallen trees seem like nothing.

"Fuck!"

I spun around, wondering if I could make it back the way I'd come after all. Or maybe go back just enough to circle the jackstraw. The only thing that greeted me was a pulsing orange through the trees, and a blast of blistering wind in my face. If I turned back now, if I ran into the wind, I'd be dead in seconds. If I pressed forward, I'd be trapped in a nest of fuel and be dead in minutes. If I stayed, I'd be dead in several fewer minutes.

"Natalie! River!" I screamed, knowing it was likely pointless. Between the fire and whatever distance they were away, River and Natalie probably couldn't hear me. Shouting was a waste of energy. Logic said River would've gone downhill; we'd grown up hearing the adage that the only things that can run faster uphill than down are fires and bears. The best way out for me was to do the same. Except that would be taking me away from River and Natalie. The best way to *maybe* find them was to attempt to cut a diagonal across the terrain as I went down and hope we crossed paths before the fire caught up.

With a vague plan and no answer to my shout, I turned and dove into the maze of fuel. I tried not to let my thoughts slow down my movements, to let my instincts guide me. If I thought about this too much I knew I'd slip, fall, twist an ankle, impale myself on a sharp branch.

Jump.

Step.

Roll.

Swing.

Everything became something to hold onto. Even tufts of tall grass provided a bit more stability for a leap from one spot to another. I was so deep into it now I wasn't even touching the ground at all, skipping and sliding along old trunks, praying not to fall.

My lungs ached in the growing smoke as I scrambled through the fallen trees, attempting to arc around the bottom of the fire in vaguely the direction Natalie and River had gone. But with how quickly the fire was going, and how deep into a bad spot I'd gotten, I wasn't even sure what I was doing now other than trying to save myself.

River was smart enough to know the right things to do here, she had good instincts and listened whenever the firefighters came to school. Problem was, with something like this, with a fire growing this fast, there might not be any right things at all.

My feet struggled for purchase as I scrambled through, many of the logs long ago stripped of their rough bark by the weather, leaving nothing but smooth wood behind. Hiking boots were meant for walking, not for a life-or-death race through terrain like this. I would've given anything for a set of caulks, anything to give me some real grip. But it didn't matter what I wanted, it mattered what I had. I needed to stop hoping and wishing and accept what I had.

The mess of lodgepoles seemed thinner to my left so I took a chance, shifting direction even though it would put me parallel to the fire rather than continuing to lead me down and away from it. I had to get out of the jackstraw, and going left would take me closer to River and Natalie.

Around me everything was turning into a mess of shadows. The last of the fading daylight had lost the battle against the fire, allowing it to become the only real source of light around. It made everything jump and twist. I reached for a log only for it to slip away, a trick of the light, and went sprawling forward, my heart in my chest as I fell, hands flailing out in search of something, anything, to arrest my momentum. Nothing was there, and I slammed into the ground face first, one leg still hooked up behind me in the crook of a branch.

Spitting out dirt, I pushed up onto my hands, trying to get enough purchase to free my foot. Was the roaring in my ears adrenaline or the fire? I couldn't tell anymore.

A few yanks pulled my foot free and I stumbled back upright, wondering if I was injured but unable to tell. I was out of the deadfall, though. Most of it, anyway.

Turning back downhill, I took off again, glad my leg didn't give out underneath me.

The mountain wasn't done, though, and without warning I once again found myself sprawled on the ground, on my back with no idea how I got there. The sky above me was nothing except crisscrossing branches and roiling smoke dotted with stars made of embers. Only when I made it up did I realize what had happened. A tiny, barely there spring bubbled under my feet, turning the ground into a slippery mud pit laced with moss.

The corner of my mind that could still remember everything I knew about fire beyond "run from it" acted before I consciously caught up. My flannel was halfway off when I realized what I was doing and started doing it faster, plunging the blue cloth, torn in several places now, into the puddle at the center of the spring. Dragging it out I wrapped it around my face and head, using the sleeves to tie it into place. It might end up giving me steam burns, but I had to do something to keep the smoke out of my lungs, even for a little while. A thorn caught in the fabric dug into my cheek, but I didn't have time to care. With several careful steps I was back on dry ground and running again.

The fire had a taste now, even through the damp cloth. It was stinging, acidic, settling in the back of my throat and staying there. I wasn't sure I could scream for Natalie and River again even if I wanted to, and I wasn't sure how long I could keep running either. Adrenaline was a finite thing. Just because I was an athlete didn't mean I had unlimited reserves. Already the awareness of injuries I hadn't felt before was starting to creep in, so many of them building up my mind could no longer ignore any of them. My eyes watered, blinking uncontrollably in an attempt to clear the smoke that bit at them. My palms stung, probably bled. My legs ached not just from exertion but from being slammed over and over again into solid wood, and the leg that had been caught when I fell the first time had a searing pain in the hip.

Wind continued to press at my back. I had to bite back a volley of swears I didn't have the breath for when a finger of fire I'd been following on my left surged forward with new vigor. Of all the races I'd run, this one was the worst because I knew losing was the only outcome, and the consequences would be so much worse than a disappointed coach.

The trail of flames crackled and spat, chewing through the sunbaked plants and old wood. It was only a few yards across, but in seconds it dashed ahead faster than I could ever hope to go. I didn't dare look back to see where the main body of the fire was. It was better not knowing.

A little voice in my head told me I was going to die alone now. That I was never going to see Iris again.

Iris.

I hoped with everything I had that she and Toby hadn't come back. That they'd called in the fire and kept going. It was a vain hope, though. Toby may have been cowardly enough to leave us behind, but Iris wasn't. She would come back.

"Don't die for me," I pleaded in my thoughts. "Go home. Don't die for me."

Captain Henderson: Where's my spot weather report?

Troublesome Dispatch: Just got it. Spot weather for the Lost Hen campground area. Winds out of the west gusting up to fifty-two miles-per-hour, no major shifts currently predicted. 42% humidity decreasing overnight. Current temperature eighty-two degrees. Predicted low for the night is seventy-one. Visibility ten miles.

Captain Henderson: Damn. We need it colder.

Troublesome Dispatch: Sir, that wind is going to push it right at the mine and probably the Village. We need to issue an evac notice for both.

Captain Henderson: Do it. Now. Send out a Code Red through the county app and a reverse 911 too.

Troublesome Dispatch: Yes, Sir.

Captain Henderson: Do we know yet if the guys in the trucks have working radios with our frequencies?

Troublesome Dispatch: Jenny's working on it. The dispatch phones are all clogged, she's using her own. We'll let you know.

Captain Henderson: Call Elliot, his number's pinned on my board.

Troublesome Dispatch: We're trying, his line's busy and he's not answering on the radios right now.

Captain Henderson: Keep trying.

CHAPTER 8: THE VILLAGE

Adam

The road down from the mine was not one meant for speed, let alone speed in a large, top-heavy truck full of water. Not to mention the fact the thing was three times the size of anything I'd driven before. I was forced to slow to a crawl on several of the curves to negate the risk of rolling myself off the road and down the embankment. Every slowdown I hit made my knuckles tighten painfully on the wheel, old flaking and cracked leather biting into my skin. On the straightaways I fiddled with the radio, rolling it through all the frequenciess to see if I could pick anything up about what was happening. Silence and static were all I found. I honestly wasn't even sure the thing worked.

It was hard to remember I needed to be slow, desperation hammering inside my skull, and I took the last turn onto the highway faster than I should have. The feel of the truck rocking a bit too far into the motion laced up my leg from the pedals, but a quick jerk of the wheel put me back where I needed to be. There'd be some new ruts in the dirt from where the tires dug in, but it didn't matter. By tomorrow it'd be lucky if there was a road at all.

"—East, gusting up to thirty-mile—42% humidity dec—is seventy-one."

I snatched the mic for the CB off the clip on the dashboard. "Hello? This is Adam Delgado from the mine, heading towards the fire in a water truck. Does anyone copy?"

Silence greeted me and I cursed, repeating the statement to no avail. I didn't know a damn thing about radios beyond the fact that signals could easily be blocked by terrain, and there was all sorts of that around. There'd be no counting on the radio for help, not the one in this old truck and with my lack of knowledge.

"Adam, it's Shawn!" a voice suddenly crackled back.

I pressed down on the mic again, relief loosening my shoulders. At least someone could hear me. While I'd gone down onto the sage flats at the base of the mountain, Shawn had gone down and then back up Gulch Road. He was higher and thus, hopefully, able to get a better signal.

"I picked up a bit from the firefighters, I think. Did you hear it?" I asked.

"Weather report," Shawn radioed back. "Tried to talk to them but I don't think they heard me."

"Where are you?" I asked.

"Halfway up Gulch. This old girl ain't too fond of the grade." His voice was tight, even through the layer of static. I couldn't imagine what it felt like to listen to the engine growl and struggle when all he wanted to do was get to his son.

"I'm just crossing the big culvert," I told him. "Might lose you until you make it over the top. Keep trying the firefighters, I'm barely picking anything up down here."

"Got it."

I hung the mic back up and shifted into a higher gear. The road curved more gently here, giving me the chance for a precious bit of speed. Coming around the last ridge before the Village gave me my first good look at the fire since I'd left the mine. I couldn't see flames, but the smoke plume was enormous. It billowed up, roiling and black until it fuzzed out into a flatter layer before pluming again, reaching up thousands of feet high and stretching towards the mine. The upper half could've been any cloud at sunset; soft white tufts in a watercolor of oranges and pinks. Underneath it was dark, the only colors shades of sickly gray. If Dante and his friends were really up there, really under that thing and surrounded by the flames that created it....

I shoved the thought out of my mind, downshifting to make the turn up County Road 32 towards the Village.

It was a small neighborhood, only a dozen or so houses

surrounded by scraggly Douglas firs and sage. All but two of the families who lived there worked at the mine. I knew most of them, if not by name then by sight. At least three of the houses, maybe more, had kids, and then there were the bunkhouses occupied by dozens of people. Several residents had horses and other animals too. All told, there were probably fifty or more people in the Village. Fifty stubborn miners and mountain people.

One of the houses with people who didn't work at the mine belonged to an eighty-nine-year-old man and his wife, Marcus and Alice Heywood, who'd lived there for sixty years. They always brought fresh baked goods to our break room, calling us their grandkids. Marcus was a veteran—of what was never quite clear, but a veteran nonetheless. I had a sinking feeling that getting him to leave was a tall order, and if he stayed then Alice stayed. If they stayed, I had no idea who else might as well.

Only one house sat on the county road itself, the rest on a road that branched off from it and circled around to rejoin it farther up. The sirens had been removed from the truck when it was decommissioned from firefighting, but it still had a damn good horn and I started beating it after making the turn onto the loop. No one seemed to be outside, probably putting their kids to bed or having a beer in front of the TV after a long day. The driveways were mostly long enough to obscure the houses somewhat, so I had no idea if I was making any impact. All I needed was one person. One person to run out and yell at me, to see the smoke so they could go warn their neighbors and I could keep going.

Finally, at the driveway for the fourth house, a furious looking woman stomped onto the road ahead of me and waved her arms. I vaguely recognized her from a few company barbecues. She was in jeans and boots, graying hair pulled away from her face, her back to the fire and smoke. I skidded to a stop next to her, cranking down the window as I did. She was already yelling.

"—making a racket?! It is nearly dark out! Keep this up and I'll call the co—"

"You need to evacuate the neighborhood now," I interrupted,

gesturing behind her. "There's a fire. It's growing fast. The whole mountain's going up."

She paled and turned, lips pressed thin and eyes wide. The trees hid most of what was going on, but over their crowns the top of the smoke plume was clearly visible. Except, if you didn't know, it could've just been any other cloud, the sunset masking its true nature. There was a whiff of woodsmoke on the breeze that ruffled the trees, but that was no reason to be suspicious. Most of the homes up here had stoves for heat.

"Oh god," she whispered, one hand covering her mouth. "Is it really that bad?" she asked, turning back to me.

I grimaced and nodded. "Get your family, warn the other houses, and get out. You do not have time for anything else."

"Can't you help?" she asked, gesturing at my truck.

"There's people trapped in the campgrounds," I said, packing urgency into my voice. "I have to get them."

Squaring her shoulders and taking a deep breath she nodded once, stepping back from the truck. "Okay. Keep blaring the horn to get people moving as you go."

I nodded and set the truck back into motion, leaving the window down so I could shout out it. Six more people came out to yell at me as I went. I screamed, "Fire, get out now!" at them and kept going without stopping, watching in the side view mirrors as they turned, saw the smoke, then scattered.

By the time I made it back to the county road, and back to a clear view of the smoke, the plume had already grown to touch the edges of the sky as far as I could see. A sense of hesitation seeped in, loosening my foot on the gas, the truck slowing underneath me. *Should* I stay and help the Village instead? There were more people there. Little kids. Homes. Dante and his friends...if they were in the middle of this....

The fire was still a decent way off from the Village, though. They at least had time and plenty of ways to evacuate, even if the time part of that equation was vanishing rapidly. Anyone at the campgrounds was already out of time, and there could be more people up there I didn't know about.

I unhooked the mic again, not sure if it would matter, and

attempted to reach the firefighters. "This is Adam Delgado. Miner's Village has been alerted and is evacuating. I repeat, Miner's Village has been alerted and is evacuating."

Letting the mic fall into my lap, I brought the truck back up to speed, the engine whining as the grade increased and I gained elevation. It wasn't too bad, yet, but I knew soon I'd be in much the same position as Shawn had been, the engine protesting that I was pushing too hard. He should've crested the ridge by now, though, and been heading down the other side, which meant our radios should be able to link up with nothing in between them.

"Shawn, where are you?" I radioed out.

No answer came, adding to the disquiet I felt. Even with his truck struggling, there was no reason he shouldn't have made it over the ridge by now. Hopefully the issue was with the radios, not something more sinister.

The road flattened out somewhat and when I reached the turnoff for Dirty Bird Road, which led to the Lost Hen campgrounds, I got my first look at the flames since leaving the mine. They stopped me in my tracks, the idle of the engine rumbling through my bones. Even from this distance they were terrifying, swallowing trees and whipping out into the sky higher than I thought possible. It was a solid wall of fire from the top of the ridge almost down to the creek that ran along the bottom. Wind swirled through everything, twisting spirals of sparks flickering out among the smoke. The ash fall was getting heavier, plinking against the metal of the truck and building up in the crevices of the hood.

Shakily, I grabbed the mic again. "This is Adam Delgado. I can see the fire again. Bring everything. This is bad. Bring everything."

Troublesome Dispatch: Reverse 911 and Code Red have been sent.

Captain Henderson: ETA update?

Troublesome Dispatch: 41 is—

Adam: —dam Delgado. Miner's Village —cuating. —alerted and is evacuating.

Captain Henderson: Delgado? Delgado say again. Susan, try can you raise him?

Troublesome Dispatch: I'm not getting much from him here either. I'll try and relay with the crews, maybe one of them can get him.

Captain Henderson: Do it. We gotta know where those guys are. Any new word from the mine?

Troublesome Dispatch: They've begun evacuating. The fire is spreading fast and headed their way.

Adam: This is Adam Delgado. I can see the fire again. Bring everything. This is bad. Bring everything.

Captain Henderson: Lord save us. Susan, did you get that?

Troublesome Dispatch: Yes sir. Requesting all possible aid.

911 Operator: Troublesome County 911, do you need police, fire, or EMS?

Caller: Um, well, I'm not sure. We're staying at an AirBNB and there's a bunch of smoke. We're just wondering what's going on and if we should leave?

911 Operator: What is your address?

Caller: Uhhh, I don't know, hang on. Honey, what's the address? Sorry, we're not one-hundred-percent sure. Maybe 718 County Road 31? My wife is checking.

911 Operator: If you're on 31 the fire is currently heading away from you. Please make sure of your address and check our county website for current information. If you feel unsafe at any time, do not wait for an official evacuation notice, just go.

Caller: Okay, thanks.

Troublesome   Dispatch: State,   Troublesome Dispatch.

State Dispatch: Troublesome Dispatch, State. What do you need?

Troublesome Dispatch: We're scrambling to do this official, but I'm warning you now we're likely going to need medical support at our hospital on top of the rest of the fire resources, we aren't big enough to handle the influx.

State Dispatch: Copy, we'll pass it on.

CHAPTER 9: BLOCKED OFF

Iris

Where I'd gotten signal on my phone had been on the other side of a little draw that obscured any view of the fire, but as the truck shuddered its way to the top flames flickered back into view.

"Oh Jesus," Toby whispered.

The truck stalled under me, the torrents of fire taking up every bit of focus I had, making me miss a shift. Wind still gusted east, but the fire was pushing south as well, down the slope of the dip between the two largest spur ridges off the mountain. It was likely going north as well, I realized. Racing out in an ever-widening V. My sense of time was completely gone, but I didn't need it to tell that the fire was swallowing the wilderness faster than anything I could comprehend.

"Jesus, Jesus, Jesus," Toby said. With the truck dead I could feel him shaking through the bench seat. No matter how entitled he was, even he had the good sense to be afraid now

"Jesus ain't here," I muttered, starting the truck again.

"Turn around, please turn around," Toby begged.

I shifted up a gear, pushing the truck a bit faster, my eyes dancing up and down between looking out the windshield and watching my RPMs on the dash. It was hard to get a good look at the dial, though, as it jumped and jostled. River's truck didn't have the best shocks under normal circumstances and with this treatment it felt like riding a bull. I'd only ridden one twice, and it was taking the same strength to hold the wheel as it did the rope around a bull's chest, the only thing holding me in place as it twisted and bucked.

"Iris, come on! Turn around. Turn around!"

We were above the fire now and I knew, *knew*, that was a horrid place to be. But as long as the wind stayed in our favor, as long as it kept blowing from the west to the east and shoving the fire down, we might have enough time. There wasn't even that much smoke up here. Out the driver's side window the forest was untouched, twilight purples and blues splashed by flickering orange.

Looking out the passenger side window provided a much different view, however. The fire seemed to have developed two layers. One raced through the duff and leaf litter on the forest floor, the other jumped and skipped from treetop to treetop. For now, both layers were at a distance, more interested in the trees and their underbrush than the scraggly plants along the road. Except it wouldn't be long before we were back in those trees.

"Iris, please. I don't want to die. *Please*." A quick glance showed me his whole body was vibrating, hands clenching and unclenching at his sides.

"Do you think Dante, River, and Natalie *do* want to die?" I exploded. "Because they are out there, right now, in the fire you fucking started. They don't even have a truck. They don't have anything. *Because of you*."

"I didn't mean to!" he retorted, shrinking away from me towards the door.

"No, Toby, you didn't *care*. You thought you were special and smart and didn't need to listen to every single person around you, to every weather and fire expert that has been on the news for *months* telling us how high the fire danger is, how it's getting worse and worse every year." Somehow, talking helped. It forced me to stay in the present, to not overthink my driving, so I kept going. "Look at this. Look out the windows. It's been, what, twenty minutes? Thirty? How many acres do you think this is already? Do you see the direction it's going? What happens when it reaches the Village? All those people, those *kids* who chased us up the road? And the mine! Half the county works there, what happens if it burns down? And all the other damn cabins out here! The Gazette Ranch! The tourists there, the one-hundred-eight horses, and hundreds, thousands of other animals!"

Toby curled forward, head wrapped up between his arms, elbows resting on his knees, refusing to look outside or at me. He rocked back and forth, but that might've just been the jolting of the truck.

Before I could lash out at him again a tree fell into the road sixty yards ahead, flames dancing along its length. A shower of sparks exploded out as it impacted the dirt, fluttering up into the sky until they burned out. Toby's head smacked against the dashboard when I hit the brakes. I didn't feel a drop of sympathy. Let him get a concussion. He deserved worse.

He straightened up and peered out the windshield, staring at the tree. Braking distance and my delayed response had brought us within twenty yards of it.

"There's no way we can drive through that," he declared. The relief in his voice made me want to hit him again.

"Fucking watch me," I snarled, hitting the button to release the winch and grabbing the fire extinguisher from the passenger footwell before wrenching my door open.

Toby sat there, mouth wide open, and didn't move to help as I went around to the front of the truck. Wind pulled at my clothes, my hair. I shouldn't have taken down the ponytail that Dante'd put it in. Leaning the extinguisher against the bumper I grabbed the winch hook and started pulling the cable out hand over hand until I had enough length. With a little finagling, I got the extinguisher ready and settled in my left hand in a way that, though uncomfortable, allowed me to both aim the nozzle and pull the trigger with just one hand. Scooping up the hook in my other one, I dashed for the tree, knowing the heat would force me back if I wasn't fast enough. Once I was within range I started blasting, aiming the jet of retardant out in low, sweeping arcs along part of the tree.

An angry hiss came from the wood, the flames vanishing in a billow of smoke and retardant, exposing five feet of charred bark. I tossed the hook and cable over the top, kneeling so fast my kneecaps screamed when they hit the dirt. Shoving one arm through a gap under the trunk, I slid my arm back and forth, grabbing for the cable to pull it back around. My cheek was pressed up against the still hot charcoal, the remains of the retardant dripping down along my forehead. The flames were coming back, crawling closer and closer to my face, burning away the retardant that had stopped them before.

My hand snagged against a ridged line and I twisted my fingers around it, falling back to pull it under the tree. A quick snap of the hook against the line and the loop of cable was secure. Scrabbling back, my face stinging from heat, I grabbed the extinguisher and made for the truck. The door still hung open and Toby still cowered in the passenger seat. Tossing the extinguisher in I swung into the cab, flipping the switch for the winch as I went, rocking in my seat and drumming the dash with one palm to egg it on.

"Come on girl," I urged. "Come on."

The line went taut and I felt the truck lurch forward a few inches. I pressed my foot against the brake, begging the tree to move. Fire had come back along the full length of it now, sprawling over the cable. I didn't know what sort of heat the metal could withstand, and I didn't want to find out. When all the tree did was dig into the dirt I sent the truck into reverse, lending the power of the engine to the winch. The truck fishtailed, sliding side to side on the road, the frame groaning.

"Come on!" I screamed.

With a jolt the tree broke in half, the part blocking the road sliding free of its position. I nearly lost control of the truck, barely managing to gain it back before we went off the road. Continuing backward, I dragged the tree until it was moved enough for us to get around. Even with the fire creeping closer out the passenger side, even with the terror of our friends being lost, I gave a little whoop of joy at the success.

Grabbing the extinguisher once more I got back out, intending to go free the cable, but was brought up short in front of the hood at the sound of a different engine from somewhere behind us. It was much louder than River's truck but still had the distinctive growl of a diesel. I saw the headlights first, obscuring all but a silhouette of the vehicle. It was big and boxy with a row of lights along the top of the cab as well as massive headlights, and a huge, reinforced silver bumper.

It waited for it to stop and dashed to the passenger side. I wanted to cry now that I could really see it, the beautiful sight of a firetruck the best thing I'd ever seen, all red and chrome. Except that's all it was. There was no white striping, no "Call 911 in an Emergency" stickers. Just a white square on the door with bold black letters giving the name of the mine and its phone number. My heart dropped.

Whoever was driving cranked down the window and I stepped forward to see them better.

"Adam?" I stuttered out.

I knew him. He was from our school, had been in my biology class my freshman year. Dante tutored him. His face was grim, brows knotted together under the rim of a hardhat. One hand rested on the edge of the window as he leaned out, a bit above me, a worried but determined look in his eyes.

He wasn't a fireman.

But he did have a firetruck.

"Iris! Who's with you?" he asked, an edge of urgency in his voice. A curl of hair that he didn't seem to notice fluttered against his forehead. From within the cab I heard the crackle of voices over a radio saying something about 911 calls.

"Do you have water in that?" I demanded, gesturing to the back.

"Yes, *who is with you?*"

"Just Toby. Dante, River, and Natalie are out there somewhere." I raced through an explanation of how we'd gotten split up.

"Okay, I'll find them. Turn around and get out of here," Adam said, acting like this was an order I was supposed to follow.

"*Excuse me?*" I said. "I'm getting in your truck and coming with you."

He shook his head. "There's only so much room in here. If I find them or anyone else I'll be their only way out. You have a vehicle. You need to take it and go."

"Four eyes are better than two!"

"Well then it's a good thing Dante's dad is coming up the other side from Gulch Road in another water truck," Adam returned.

I stared at him, and he stared back.

"I can't leave," I pleaded. "They need help."

Adam swallowed, glancing out at the forest. The fire was still held back by the wind, but it was getting ever closer, determined to climb the hill. The tree that had blocked us was the only close one burning so far, but it wouldn't be for long.

"The Village needs help too," Adam said, attention back on me. "Go help them."

I didn't want him to be right even though I knew he was. Taking up a seat in his cab when I had my own way out would be wrong. My shoulders dropped and I nodded.

He nodded back, asking me what Dante, River, and Natalie were wearing and where I'd last seen them. I told him everything, then watched as he drove off. Glancing back at River's truck I saw Toby pressed against the window, watching with wide eyes. Flipping him off I used the extinguisher to douse the tree again, freeing the cable.

Back in the cab, I mashed the switch to reel in the cable, my whole body shaking, jaw aching from how tight I was clenching it.

"What's happening?" Toby asked.

"We're leaving," I said through my teeth. "Adam is going to get the others."

Toby wilted against the door. "Oh thank god, thank god. Let's go!"

A little sob escaped my lips. I didn't have the energy to yell at him anymore. The thunk of the hook against the winch housing indicated it was fully wound. My hands shaky on the wheel and gear knob, I maneuvered the truck back and forth until we were turned around. Tears began to roll one by one down my cheeks. I didn't bother to wipe them away as they dripped into my lap.

@Market8282
Yo, anyone see that smoke plume southeast of town? It biiiiiiig.
↻ 5 | ♥ 6

> **@AyyyyyyUp**
> Oh snap.
> ↻ 0 | ♥ 0

@HorseRunner74
My boyfriend just called me from the mine. A big fire started. Praying for everyone there and all the firefighters. #LostHenFire
↻ 32 | ♥ 56

> **@AlleyBookGal**
> I can't believe it! My wife and I were just up there camping with the kids last weekend! Terrible.
> ↻ 0 | ♥ 1

@JessicaLostIt
Please, does anyone know the exact location of the fire? My parents live in Miner's Village! #LostHenFire #MinersFire #Help
↻ 1 | ♥ 3

@TroubleCoFire
Alert: new fire start in the area of the Lost Hen Campground. Currently unknown acreage. Evacuation notice issued for Miner's Village. Pre-evac issued for other structures in area. Go to county website for most up-to-date info. #LostHenFire
↻ 24 | ♥ 34

@HorseRunner74

Stay safe guys! We're rooting for you.

↻ 2 | ♥ 14

@JessicaLostIt

Please go check on house 214 in Miner's Village! Please! My dad's too stubborn to leave! Please! He and my mom aren't answering their phones! Their names are Marcus and Alice Heywood!

↻ 0 | ♥ 1

@RickyTheMovieBuff

How far is it from the village? The mine?

↻ 0 | ♥ 0

@RickyTheMovieBuff

Helllllllloooo? Anyone going to bother to answer? How far is it from the Village? The mine?

↻ 0 | ♥ 0

Troublesome Dispatch: Crews be aware, 911 is jammed with reports, even state dispatch. We may be missing crucial calls. We're getting through them as fast as possible. Any department listening, send everyone you have. Fire. EMS. Police. We're going to need it all.

Middle Park Dispatch: Troublesome County, this is Middle Park County. We've got six engines and every officer we have heading your way. ETA one hour.

Troublesome Dispatch: Amanda? That you?

Middle Park Dispatch: Yeah, just got called in.

Troublesome Dispatch: Sorry, I'm on the verge of tears. We can't find enough help.

Middle Park Dispatch: Hang in there honey, we'll get through this. Take it one call at a time.

@TroubleCoFire

911 is currently overwhelmed. If you have an emergency not related to the #LostHenFire, please call Sadie's Hill Church at 970-555-6892. They have stepped in as a backup dispatch center.

⟳ 104 | ♥ 29

@Rittenburger

Illegal, lol. Hope the fire burns down your whole town.

⟳ 0 | ♥ 0

@AlleyBookGal

Go away. You clearly aren't from here. They're doing everything they can.

⟳ 28 | ♥ 22

@Rittenburger

Aww, is someone triggered? Do you need a safe space? Maybe try Lost Hen, I hear it's very warm this time of year.

⟳ 0 | ♥ 0

CHAPTER 10: FALLING

Dante

The water soaking my flannel had evaporated completely, leaving the fabric to scratch roughly against my skin. At least it hadn't burned me, as far as I could tell. On its own, without the moisture, it wasn't doing nearly as much to help with the smoke. I could barely keep my eyes open, the instinct to blink away the stinging clouds at total odds with my need to keep my footing. It felt a lot like trying to avoid falling asleep in the car; a continual denial of what my body needed no matter how many times my head bobbed up and down, no matter how many times my eyes tried to close.

Fire swirled around me on all sides. The race was lost. Done. Any advantage I had from football, from endless hours at the gym, had long bled away. Each step became harder, my limbs heavier every time, my feet less sure as they came back down. It didn't even surprise me when the world pitched sideways.

No instinct welled up, no memory of how to take a fall, no snapping my arms forward to protect my face from grinding into the dirt. At least the flannel kept my skin from getting peeled off when I hit, rocks and dirt scraping away the skin on my arms instead. Though, it didn't really matter if my face got messed up, did it? I was about to burn to death. It wasn't like I was going to get an open casket funeral.

I didn't get up, the word "funeral" knocking back and forth in my skull. Why had it come so easily? I hadn't given up yet... had I?

No. No way.

I just. Had to get up. Keep going.

Why wasn't I getting up? Why wouldn't my body listen?

Funeral. Funeral. Funeral.

Get up. Get up. Get up.

Funeral. Funeral. Funeral.

GET UP.

I managed to roll onto my stomach from where I'd landed on my side, arranging my arms to try and push up from there. Little stones bit into my palms, but my hands slipped out from under me.

Was it the smoke? It must be the smoke. Stealing away the air I needed to function.

I couldn't get up.

Funeral. Funeral. Funeral.

Burying my face into the crook of my elbow I tried to ignore everything, the suffocating smoke, the dreadful heat, the blaring roar. Push it down, just like the noise of the crowd and the glare of the lights at a game. Maybe I'd get lucky and suffocate before I burned. That would be good. Burning seemed like a terrible way to go.

I wondered what picture my parents would put on top of the casket instead of having it open. Maybe they'd use one that Iris took. She always took good pictures, even if they were just with her phone. My smiles with her were real, not staged like in my yearbook photos.

I wanted to see the world one more time, I realized. Something beautiful. Something alive. Something I could touch. Something green. My limbs wouldn't move at all now, though. It took five tries before I struggled up to my elbows, the movements jolting and shaky. Every muscle in my arms and shoulders screamed to give up, to lie back down.

When I managed to look around, there was nothing alive for comfort. Only flames. Something in my mind slowed everything down and I marveled at the coiling, dancing shapes, the elegant curves and steady gradients of color. It wasn't the beauty I'd wanted, but it was still beautiful. Even as someone who'd studied a multitude of fires, determined to grow up to be a firefighter since I was three, I could appreciate the awe of its destruction. My destruction.

I wanted to see all of it, I realized. Wanted to know what was coming. I was going to roll over onto my back, stare up into the sky, and watch.

Pushing up a bit farther, it occurred to me the motion didn't take as much energy as before. Sluggishly my brain supplied the reason why: oxygen. There was more air, cooler air, near the ground. It happened all the time in fires. People fell down, only to be revived somewhat by the better air lower down, allowing them to carry on just a bit longer. My eyes still stung and watered, awareness bleeding back in of their pain and all the other pains. Awareness of my surroundings. There were no plants under my palms. No flames were touching me. Nothing but ten feet of pockmarked dirt spread out ahead of me.

Oh.

I turned my head left and right to be sure, finding that my assumption was correct. I was on the road. That was probably good. I could run faster on the road. There wasn't fire on the road.

But which way? Right, south, went back up the mountain, straight into the heart of the fire, so that was out. Left went down, but first it also went into the fire. There were switchbacks, so it would turn around eventually, I just didn't know when, or how many more switchbacks there were. Plus, before it switched back, it would lead me deeper into the gulch. Gulches were bad. Why were gulches bad? They were...they were...wind, maybe? Chimneys. They made chimneys. Funneled the fire in unexpected directions. Pushed it faster. Storm King. Mann Gulch. Yarnell. Firefighters had died in gulches in those fires, I thought. I'd read about them, but the details were fuzzy. What had the after action reports said about how they might have survived?

The answer didn't come to me before the world suddenly, painfully snapped back into focus. I yelped, rolling away from the pain. A glance at my right shoulder showed me a burned, smoldering hole about the size of a golf ball in my shirt, the skin underneath an angry pink and white.

Not giving myself time to fall back into confusion and

exhaustion, I fought up to my feet, turning left and using whatever I had to start running. Deeper into the gulch or not, I'd be faster on the road.

The switchback came up sooner than I expected, sending a trickle of relief through me. Once I rounded it I'd be heading out of the gulch again. Unless there was another one after it.

No.

Just keep running. One foot in front of the other.

Get out. Get out. Get out.

This was nothing more than a drill on the field before a game, yards disappearing under my feet. One, two, three, ten, fifteen.

Get out. Get out.

Twenty. Thirty.

Get out.

Fifty.

A shower of embers exploded down the road, something bursting out of the trees and forcing me to stop. My aching eyes couldn't parse the shapes roiling in front of me. Browns and blacks, long angular branches whipping around. Whatever it was was huge. And screaming.

"Elk," I realized with dawning horror, unsure if I said it aloud or in my head.

There were maybe a dozen of them, bodies slamming together, heads thrown back as they wailed. It was clear that they didn't want to run back into the fire on either side of the road, but they were also too panicked to figure out they could run down the road. Instead they ran in circles, slamming into one another over and over, their fear killing them just as much as the flames.

One of them, a bull with long, spear-sharp antlers arcing back from his skull, was on fire. The image didn't seem real, seem possible. Flames danced along his whole back, sending up showers of sparks with every movement he made, every slam of another member of the herd into his body.

How wasn't he falling down?

Wait.

When had I fallen down?

I was on my knees, mesmerized by the scene unfolding before me. My head felt like a boulder as I rolled it side to side, looking around and trying to figure out what to do. The ember hitting my shoulder, the painful awareness and burst of energy it brought, were gone. So was the boost I'd gained from getting a little more oxygen at ground level.

The elk were blocking the road, still swirling in panic. Maybe they'd come this way. Getting trampled didn't seem nice. Their hooves were sharp. No, I didn't want to get trampled. But the elk were blocking the road. And the forest on either side was on fire. But the elk were blocking the road. Was burning or trampling better? Maybe I could find another clear spot to lay down. Off the road. Yeah. Then I'd just suffocate. That would be okay.

This was just a dream, after all. That's why I couldn't move right. That's why my limbs were filled with lead. No one could run in dreams. That was how dreams worked.

Now I was standing. I didn't remember standing.

What a crappy dream. Iris was going to laugh at me when I told her. The big bad future smokejumper, scared by a dream. Ridiculous. She'd let me fall back asleep with my head in her lap, though, so I didn't have the dream again. That would be nice. Really nice.

Elliot: This is Elliot at the mine. We're nearly evacuated. The fire isn't laying down, and it's running hard. It'll be over the ridge between us and the ignition point any minute now.

Captain Henderson: Elliot, what's your assessment on fighting it? Can you see anywhere to cut a line?

Elliot: No. Not tonight. It's moving too fast. We need to get everyone and get out of the way.

Shawn: Elliot, it's Shawn, you copy?

Elliot: I hear you. Where are you? Have you found the kids?

Shawn: No. Found a family whose car went into a ditch. Had to pull them out. Back on my way now, almost to the top of the ridge.

Elliot: Radio the second you reach the top. Tell us what the fire's doing on the other side.

Shawn: Copy.

Captain Henderson: Anyone heard from the other guy? Delgado?

Elliot: Not since he called out to bring everything. The radio in his truck is janky, the speakers aren't connected well.

Captain Henderson: How many are evacing the mine?

Elliot: One-hundred-twelve. I'll be last out in our remaining water truck.

Captain Henderson: Which way are you sending people out?

Elliot: West on the highway. Towards Sadie's Hill and against the wind. If I send them down to Moose Lake it's twice as far and they'll be going with the wind with the fire at their backs. Me and some of the other guys are going to the Village to help them evacuate.

Captain Henderson: Understood. Be smart.

@JackrabbitNightmare

Up on my buddy's roof watching the smoke plume. Gettin' scary. More the light falls more you can see the bottom glowin'. #LostHenFire

↻2 | ♥1

> **@AidenAidenAiden**
>
> You're not too close, are you? Mom'll have a fit if she finds out you're just standing around watching.
>
> ↻0 | ♥0

> > **@JackrabbitNightmare**
> >
> > Nah, I'm miles off. Still don't tell Mom...
> >
> > ↻0 | ♥0

@TroubleCoFire

Alert: If you are within five miles of Lost Hen on to the east and north you are under mandatory evacuation. Five miles after that is under pre-evac. More info on the county site. #LostHenFire

↻36 | ♥108

> **@JessicaLostIt**
>
> TELL ME YOU'RE CHECKING ON HOUSE 214 IN MINER'S VILLAGE! 911 ISN'T ANSWERING! PLEASE! I'M TWO STATES AWAY.
>
> ↻5 | ♥3

@HellaHighMusic

"Get an AirBNB in the mountains for your honeymoon," they said. "It'll be romantic," they said. Yeah right. So much smoke our eyes are watering. Guess we're on the safe side of it, tho?

↻ 0 | ♥ 0

@HellaHighMusic

"Get an AirBNB in the mountains for your honeymoon," they said. "It'll be romantic," they said. Yeah right. So much smoke our eyes are watering. Guess we're on the safe side of it, tho?

911 Operator: Troublesome County 911, do you need police, fire, or EMS?

Caller: I'm in Miner's Village, where's the fire department? We can see flames from our house now.

911 Operator: We're going as fast as we can, ma'am, they're almost there. If you can see flames you need to leave.

Caller: They're still a ways off, though. I think we're okay if the firefighters will be here soon.

911 Operator: Ma'am, I am advising you that you need to leave. It will be easier on our crews to only have to worry about structures, not lives.

Caller: No, no, I think we're alright. Thank you.

911 Operator: Ma'am, you need to leave. Ma'am? Ma'am? Damn. Lost her.

CHAPTER 11: CAMPGROUND

Adam

Finding Iris and Toby had sent a balloon of hope up through my chest. Finding out they were alone popped it. Finding out the other three were on foot wrapped a band around my chest, squeezing it tight.

Iris had looked heartbroken at my demand to leave. I hoped that giving her the mission of helping the Village would be enough to keep her from coming back. The clunky old truck she was in wouldn't have stood a chance against this onslaught. Toby, though, hadn't even got out of the truck, and I wondered why. I didn't really know the guy at all, small town or not. Maybe he was hurt. Maybe that would give Iris more reason not to come back.

A shift in the wind sent so much smoke across the road looking out the windshield became useless. There was nothing but undulating gray backlit by the glow of the fire. Gritting my teeth I slowed, edging the truck over to the left side of the road, against the hill and away from the slope on the other side. Pressing my head against the driver's window, I stared through the haze, finding the edge of the road from there as I continued to steer.

Soon tendrils of fire joined the smoke, jumping in and out of view among the gray. There was no way they weren't hitting the truck. I just had to hope they weren't doing any serious damage.

Random words dribbled out of the radio, stringing together a grim picture but an incomplete one. Elliot was there a few times, and Shawn was once. None of the other voices were recognizable through the static.

"Screw regulations—ater drop—structures."

"Wind incr—up to 80—"

"41 nearly the—"

"—cutting a line around the Vill—"

All at once I cleared the top of a small rise and the smoke vanished. Wisps of it still lingered, tossed about on the wind with flakes of fluffy white ash, but the solid bank was gone. The fire was too. My headlights washed out over a landscape turned black. Pines were stripped and spindly, silent sentries on an abandoned battlefield. Any plants on the ground had been obliterated, ash and soot the only remnants of their existence. A few flames lingered, little palm-sized creatures nibbling at the dregs left behind. Down the hill the main fire still raged, angrier and more expansive than before, pushing forward in search of more fuel.

Rolling down my window I shouted, "Dante! River! Natalie!"

No answer came.

Leaving the window down, I kept going. With the landscape decimated, I wasn't quite sure where I was. The campground Iris had told me they were at couldn't be much farther, I just had to make sure I didn't miss it among the unrecognizable landscape. It was the last one before the road turned downhill, heading for the bottom of the gully where it reconnected with County Road 32, which would hopefully make it easy enough to spot.

The tires kicked up ash and soot as I bumped along, a cloud of it visible in the side-view mirrors. Some trees lay across the road. So far they were all small. Nothing I was afraid to drive this big, reinforced truck over.

"Dante! River! Natalie!"

No answer, still.

"This is Adam, anyone copy?" I tried over the radio. Again, no answer.

It was starting to feel like I was the last man alive in an apocalypse. Was the fire still running hard? Which way? How fast? There was no way to tell from this side.

I almost missed the little spur road that led to the right campground, the form of it faded out without plants to indicate the edges. An outcropping of rock with a metal post sticking out of it, a warped and unreadable metal sign still screwed to the top, was all that kept me from passing by.

When I reached a clearing that seemed like a campsite I put the truck in park, slipping out of my polyester safety vest before hopping out. Plastic clothing seemed like a bad idea, under the circumstances. I kept the hardhat on, though.

There was nothing left around me but ruin. If it weren't for two reddish puddles of melted plastic next to the remains of a fire ring, I wouldn't have realized this was a campsite at all. Approaching them, my boot snagged on a long, thin stick. No. A piece of tent pole. How it hadn't melted eluded me.

Just south of the campsite, only a short distance from the fire ring, stood one pine tree that seemed a touch blacker, the char a bit deeper. Embers still glowed in the cracks of its trunk.

I cupped my hands around my mouth. "Dante! River! Natalie!"

Silence.

Deciding to try something else, I climbed back into the truck and laid on the horn a few times. Standing on the entry step, one hand on the Oh Shit handle inside the cab and one on the top of the door, I listened.

Silence, save for the distant roar of the flames. No voices calling out for help. No screams.

Either they weren't close enough to hear me, or they weren't capable of responding. Neither was a comforting possibility.

Which way would they have run? Iris said River and Natalie had gone northeast from the campsite, thus Dante must've as well. Would they have had time to run up the ridge and drop down the other side of it, or had the fire cut them off, forcing them down?

"—hawn, who copies?"

I scrambled back into the truck, snatching up the mic. "Shawn, it's Adam. I hear you, do you hear me?"

"I hear you, Adam."

"I'm at the campsite where Dante and his friends were," I said, rushing through the words in case the radio dropped out. "I found two, Iris and Toby. They're heading down in an old red

Ford. Looking for Dante, River, and Natalie now. They're not at the campsite. Iris said they're on foot."

Shawn made a pained noise. "I just reached the top of this ridge. Elliot, you listening?"

"I'm here," Elliot said.

"It's bad," Shawn said. "It's real bad."

"Tell me what you see," Elliot insisted.

"A big wall of flame all along the bottom of the gulch with a lotta little spot fires out ahead of it. It's starting to climb the hill, and it's coming quick."

"Is it coming at you?" I asked.

"Yeah."

"Shawn, get outta there," Elliot demanded.

"Like hell, my son is in there somewhere."

"Shawn, the fire's out on my side. I'll follow it down from behind. I'll find him. Elliot is right, turn around, you'll be driving straight into if you don't," I insisted.

No answer came.

"Shawn?" Elliot called. "Shawn?"

"I'm going," he said.

"Shawn, no! Your son wouldn't want you to die for him," Elliot said.

Shawn didn't answer.

"Shawn," I tried.

He still didn't answer.

"Fuck all. Adam, are you sure you can follow it safely?" Elliot asked.

I debated, staring down into the flames. They were not going out as fast as they were apparently going forward on the other side. If I went down the hill it wouldn't be long until I was back in the worst of it.

"Yeah, I'm sure," I lied. I hadn't seen them on the way in, so if I was going to find them it would mean going forward.

If Dante, River, and Natalie were out here, the road was their best chance, and I had to believe they'd know that. Dante would, at least. Half the tutoring sessions we had were timed around his volunteering at the station. Maybe I'd find the three of them on the road, maybe I wouldn't, but I certainly wasn't going to find them if I turned around.

"Don't make me pay for your funeral, you hear me?" Elliot said. "I'm about to leave the mine. May lose contact."

"Understood," I told him.

Getting back out, I circled the truck once, checking for damage. Ash buffeted me in a renewed wind, making it hard to get a whole picture. The paint, already chipped and scuffed, was bubbling in some spots, the rubber grip pads on the steps up to the cab had warped and were hanging off in places, all that remained of the mudflaps was their metal hinges, and there was soot and ash packed in every crevice. The tires were all still holding air, except...that might not be entirely good.

Opening the passenger door I riffled through the glove box, relieved when I found a little tire gauge. Kneeling, I untwisted the cover of the valve on the front passenger tire and pressed the gauge to the opening. The plastic stick shot out way farther than it should've for these tires. Resetting it, I checked again, and a third time to be sure. The reading remained the same. The air of just the little bit of fire I'd been through had been so hot it was pushing the tires to the limit. Chances of them surviving a longer run through the flames were minimal. Still, I could buy them some more time.

Using the other end of the gauge I scrambled around, bleeding off a bit of pressure from each tire until they were slightly under-inflated. Finished, I grabbed the Oh Shit handle and swung myself up into my seat, slamming the door behind me. It took two tries to get the engine going, something I tried not to think too deeply about.

My sisters flashed across my mind, and I hesitated. They'd already lost our mom and dad three years ago, if they lost me too.... But if it was them down there, I would've given anything for someone to help them. My sisters had my aunt and uncle. Right now, Dante, River, and Natalie had no one.

Maybe I'd find them down the road. Maybe I wouldn't. But I was going.

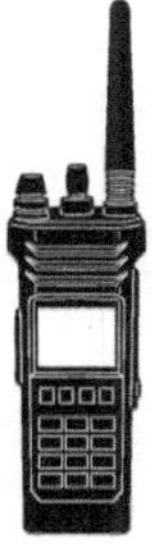

Troublesome Dispatch: All units be advised, our total potentially occupied structure count within five miles of the east side of the fire is 23. 4 of those are mine buildings which are already evacuating, 11 are houses in the Village which have been issued an evacuation notice, the rest are assorted cabins spread out across the area.

Captain Henderson: Copy.

Elliot: The wind is getting worse. You're going to need more than a five-mile radius.

Troublesome Dispatch: Understood. We'll work on it.

Captain Henderson: Elliot, all your people out yet?

Elliot: Last one just pulled out. I'm heading down too.

Captain Henderson: How many are going to the Village?

Elliot: 12, including me. Two of them live

there, the rest have trucks to help take stuff out. I made everyone else go to town. First guy in line has a list of names of who's going in. He'll pull over and hand it off when he sees someone.

Captain Henderson: Understood.

CHAPTER 12: EVACUATION

Iris

The fire galloped beside us, veering away down the mountain a little at a time, and I was struck by the inexplicable thought of riding Fiddle through the flames like some heroine in an overly CGIed movie. Fire would lick at our legs, Fiddle's nostrils would be blown wide, I'd be bent low in the saddle. Barely there horses would fade in and out around us, formed in the flames. I'd find Dante somewhere, haul him up behind me, and get us both out of there, with a very romantic kiss at the end, of course.

A delirious laugh escaped my lips. It felt a bit like choking. Maybe it was.

I could feel Toby staring at me, but he didn't say anything and I didn't feel like returning the look. Let him think he was in a truck being driven by a madwoman. Served him right.

My phone buzzed in the cup holder between us as we bumped and jostled down the mountain, but I didn't dare reach for it. Toby glanced at it, then looked around the cab.

"Wait, where's mine?" he asked, tilting up the center console to look underneath.

"In a ditch, now shut up. I'm concentrating. I don't want to stall again."

"You left my phone in a ditch?"

"Toby, do me a favor and check the glove compartment for duct tape."

"Why?"

"Because I'm going to need you to put it over your mouth."

"Oh, right, how dare I ask where *you* took *my* property."

"Please, feel free to get out and go find it."

Out of the corner of my eye I saw him glaring before his hand snaked out and snatched my phone out of the cup holder. He thumbed through the messages that had popped up during the brief connection to a signal.

"Your mom wants to know where you are," he said blandly.

"Gee, I can't imagine why. Is there still signal?"

He didn't answer and instead, without warning, leaned over the seat and held the phone in front of my face. Slamming the brakes nearly sent my face crashing into the screen and the engine died in spluttering protest. Toby was already back in his seat, now with Twitter pulled up.

"Did you just...did you just almost send us off the road to unlock *my phone with my face ID*?" I screamed, unable to believe him. It was as if the farther we got from the fire, the less he cared. Which was saying a lot, given he'd never seemed to care at all.

He didn't answer and I watched him log out of my Twitter account and into his own.

"If I thought I could live with myself, I'd leave you out here to die," I said quietly.

This got his attention, his mouth dropping open.

Restarting the truck took three tries, my hands were shaking so much.

"I texted your mom that you're okay," Toby whispered a minute later.

"Did it go through?" I said stiffly.

"Yeah. But the signal vanished right after."

"Did you bother to text everyone else's parents? Tell them their kids *aren't* fine?"

"I didn't mean to start it, Iris. You know I didn't mean to," he muttered.

"I'm sure that'll make for a great funeral speech," I said, twisting the knife deeper.

Silence fell in the cab, the only sound now the rumble of the engine and the bumping of the tires. Scores of untouched trees blurred by out my window, the only visible flames distant as they crawled up the next ridge. Sometimes even those vanished, obscured by the forest. It could've been any night. It could've been the night it was meant to. I should've been kissing Dante right now, trying to work up the courage to take off his shirt. Not wondering if he was dead.

A new sound faded in as we got closer to the Village, a clawing roar different from the fire. I couldn't place it until, just before the northernmost part of the Village, a swath of forest disappeared out my window. River was going to need new brakes if I kept slamming them like this. And a new transmission. If she lived. Please let her live.

The chunk of empty woodland was as wide as a road and covered in sawdust. Roaring chainsaws chewed through trees, wielded by six people I could see. More people on ATVs flitted back and forth, dragging downed trees away. An old man was in a backhoe, scraping everything down to the dirt. Not one person was in uniform, it was just a collection of jeans and flannel. They'd only made about fifty yards of progress.

"What are they doing?" Toby asked, leaning over the center console to get a better look.

"Cutting a firebreak," I said. Firefighting was mostly a mystery to me, but I'd picked a few things up from dating Dante.

The window stuck as I cranked it down, only making it halfway. Three heavy thumps on the horn got the attention of the closest ATV rider and she sped over to me, pulling up next to my window. She was in jeans and hiking boots, sleeves of a tattered red flannel rolled up to her elbows and graying hair pulled away from her face.

"We're busy," she said, not bothering to be pleasant.

"You need to leave," I told her. "You don't have time, and this fire is moving too fast for a single line to matter. It won't help. Please go, please."

She shook her head. "These are our homes, this is our community. We all knew living out here meant handling things ourselves. We're prepared."

"No you aren't," I insisted.

She shook her head again and pulled away, dust from her

tires drifting into the cab.

"What idiots," Toby scoffed.

All I managed this time was a screech. If the fire didn't kill me, the stress of dealing with Toby would. I knew he was rich, I knew he was entitled, I knew he had zero functional knowledge of the real world, but this utter disregard for what he'd done was beyond my comprehension.

A warning light appeared on the dash, the little low-pressure oil can symbol glowing ominously. Of course. Why not. Who needed oil pressure anyway.

With one last glance at the people trying to cut a break, lit only by headlamps and headlights, I got moving again. Any energy I had for arguing was gone, burned away by terror and anger. I'd warned them. Their fate was their own now.

The turn into the neighborhood from this direction was a sharp one, hairpinning back on itself before evening out into a gentle curve that looped around to connect all the houses. Many of the houses were set back from the road, but lights from their windows shone through the trees, indicating where they were. Shouts echoed back and forth, words snatched in a stiff gust of wind and drowned by the engines of multiple vehicles.

Without warning three horses dashed across in front of us, phone numbers painted on their sides and a young girl chasing them, urging them on. Once they were at a gallop the girl stopped, turning to look at us before jogging up to my window where I'd come to a halt.

"Clark!" I said, recognizing her frizzy, shoulder-length brown curls and wide hazel eyes from dozens of rodeos and practices. She was on the circuit with me, top of her age group in roping. She was only twelve.

"Iris? What are you doing here?" She asked, fingers curling around the glass of my window as she stood on tip toe to look around inside.

"We were camping," I said. "Clark, you and your family need to leave, *now*."

Clark glanced back in the direction she'd come from.

"We're tryin'," she said. "But Granny's bed-bound, she can't even sit up or she passes out, and dad's down in Texas with the truck. We've only got my mom's little two-door thingy."

"We'll take her," I said immediately. "Which driveway's yours?"

Clark hesitated. "It can't be that bad, Iris. Granny hates going anywhere. Mom wants to wait."

"Clark, I am telling you right now, it is worse than anything you can imagine. You and your family need to leave." If she didn't agree I was kidnapping her.

She chewed her lip, then popped the door behind me and climbed into the backseat, pointing to the driveway a few yards ahead. At the end of it stood a ragged log cabin, a newer but still old extension tacked onto one side. The place looked loved. White shutters with little flowers painted on them, chairs made out of logs scattered in the yard, tools leaned up against the walls, scrap metal sculptures dotted around. A barn with stalls for six horses sat next to the house, stall doors thrown wide, revealing their empty interiors. A few chickens were still pecking at the ground in their enclosure, no doubt roused by all the noise and commotion.

"Can your Grandma lay in the backseat, or do we need to put her in the bed?" I asked Clark, sliding out of the truck.

"I don't know," Clark said, getting out with me. "I'll get my mom."

Toby got out as well, standing awkwardly. Ignoring him, I let down the tailgate and hopped up to remove River's toolbox so there would be more room if needed. A quick glance through the contents, churned up by my earlier exploration, showed nothing that seemed sentimental. It did reveal an old two-person tent, though, the only thing that seemed like it might be useful.

Chucking the tent at Toby, I started unscrewing the bolts holding the box in place. "Set this up," I told him. "We can put Clark's Grandma inside if she needs to be back here. Keep the dust off her, at least."

Dragging the toolbox to the tailgate I pushed it off to the side, sending it tumbling into the grass. Toby just stood there, holding the tent.

"I need help carrying her," a voice said from behind us.

Turning, I saw Clark's mom, Emmy, silhouetted in her front door, poorly suppressed fear on her face. I hopped down and followed her inside, Toby trailing in my wake. A short hallway and a turn to the right led into what seemed to have once been a den but was now a hospital space. The room was cozy and personal, dozens of pictures on the walls, a worn armchair in the corner with a faded quilt draped over it. The woman in the bed was paper frail with age, fingers gnarled, and skin dotted with liver spots. Even with age, her wide eyes still looked exactly like her granddaughter's.

"Hello dears, my name is Mable. I'm sorry to be so much trouble," she said, brushing some wispy white hair out of her face.

"You're not trouble, Granny," Clark assured, patting her leg through the covers.

"How are we doing this?" I asked Emmy.

She looked around, seemingly at a loss. "Her heart's fragile, and her osteoporosis...we have to be careful. We just, we can't afford putting her in a nursing home. I'm not sure what the best way to move her would be."

"Nonsense," Mable huffed, gesturing to Toby. "This young man here seems perfectly capable of scooping little old me up out of this bed. If my heart and bones can't take a rescue then perhaps it's just my time."

"Mom," Emmy said, real fear in her voice. "Don't say that."

"Well, son, are you going to come get me or what?" Mable asked, ignoring her daughter.

Toby glanced at Emmy who huffed and threw up her hands, nodding at Toby to go ahead. Toby didn't move, his eyes wide.

"Oh for the love of—" I muttered. Stepping forward myself I pulled back Mabel's blankets and put one arm under her knees and one behind her shoulders.

"Now, there's a proper country woman!" Mable said, patting my shoulder as I gingerly lifted her up. "Though I know darn well I'm lighter than a haybale these days."

"You certainly are," I agreed. "Much prettier than one too."

She giggled and patted my cheek this time.

Measuring my steps one by one, and with Emmy's help getting down the two front stairs, we made it to the truck. Emmy climbed in and helped lower her mother down onto the backseat, deciding that was safest even if it meant her mother's legs would be curled up. Mable seemed amused by the fuss being made when Clark appeared with the quilt from the den and a pillow.

Emmy dashed back inside, Clark following. When they reappeared, Emmy had a single file box in one hand and two coats under one arm, five frames under the other. Clark had a carrier with a very displeased cat inside and a backpack. All of it got deposited on the floor of the truck in front of Mable. Clark tried to go back for the chickens as well, but Emmy wouldn't let her do more than unlatch their coop to give them a chance, saying there wasn't time.

"Get in the bed," I ordered Toby, pointing determinedly until he did as told. Assholes who started wildfires lost cab privileges when evacuees needed the seats.

Clark squeezed into the back, sitting in the remaining floorspace at her grandmother's feet, trying to shush her crying cat. Emmy took the passenger seat and we were off.

Within moments we were stopped by a wildly waving man with a toddler clutched to his side.

"My power's gone out, I can't get my car out of my garage!" he said once I rolled to a stop.

"Get in," I told him.

He didn't need to be told twice, swinging the child up next to Toby, climbing in as well. As soon as they were secure we were back in motion.

By the time we reached the county road again there were three more people in the bed, several boxes, a pile of duffel bags, and two dogs. There were more trucks with us too, each loaded much the same.

Together we rumbled out onto the highway, turning west towards town.

"Oh Lord," Emmy whispered, fingers pressing to her lips as she looked out the back window. A glance in the rearview mirror showed a wall of fire bearing down on the Village. It would be there in moments. "Jesus deliver us."

@JeepinToby
Ugh. Hate it when people are just DETERMINED to be mad at you for things that aren't even your fault.
↻ 0 | ♥ 3

911 dispatcher: Troublesome county 911, do you need police, fire, or EMS?

Caller: Hi, I called a little bit ago, my wife and are at the AirBNB—

911 dispatcher: Sir, do you have an immediate emergency?

Caller: Well, we still can't find the exact address, the internet isn't really working on our phones—

911 dispatcher: Sir, we are in the middle of a rapidly changing and dangerous fire, with dozens of calls backed up. *Do you have an immediate emergency?*

Caller: Well, we can see flames out the window now.

911 dispatcher: Then leave.

Caller: Okay, okay, but where do we go? None of these damn country roads are labeled.

911 dispatcher: I can't direct you if you don't have an address for me to check. Just proceed to the highway, other people are evacuating as well and will be able to lead you out.

Caller: Okay, thanks.

CHAPTER 12: THE POND

River

"Come on, River, come on, I've got you."

Natalie's arm was tight around me, the other firmly clasping my hand where it draped over her shoulder, dragging me along despite the minimal contribution of my own feet to our progress. My face stung, though there was still a big hole of nothing within the stinging. It felt like part of my head was just gone. Natalie definitely would've screamed if part of my head was missing, however, so it couldn't actually be gone. Also, I was not dead.

Heat blasted us from every direction now, pinpricks of it biting into my skin. Sparks, maybe? Fuck. What a horrible time to not be able to see.

My whole body wanted to give up, muscles turning to stubborn putty. No amount of urging and begging could make them do what I asked, make my feet go where I wanted. Natalie kept having to heave me back up as I slipped lower and lower. Plants snagged at my legs, tried to pull me down. Even though she wouldn't do it I wanted to tell Natalie to let me go, but my voice wasn't working any better than my legs.

"I can see the pond," Natalie gasped, hefting me a little higher once more.

"Water?" I asked, hoping she understood that I wanted to know the depth, wanted to know if this sanctuary was another thing stolen from us by the drought. When she didn't respond I realized I might not have managed to say it out loud and tried again.

"Some," Natalie said.

Some. That could mean anything. A ten-foot-deep respite or a quagmire of mud. Too bad I couldn't see for myself. Maybe there wasn't a hole in my face, maybe my eyes were gone.

The ground was flat beneath us now, which meant we must be getting close. The pond shouldn't be far from where the ground evened out.

The lack of slope didn't make it any easier to walk, though. One of my feet caught on the heel of the other, sending us stumbling. To her credit, Natalie managed to keep us from falling, though the action wrenched my shoulder painfully.

"Nice catch," I praised, the words painful. A little giggle I couldn't control bubbled up out of my throat after them, stinging even more.

"You're in shock," she returned.

Her voice was raspy. I didn't like it. All the warm honey tones were gone.

Under my boots the ground began to get softer, sucking my soles back down when I tried to lift my feet. This was too much for my remaining coordination, my legs twisting into a pretzel once again and refusing to untangle this time. Natalie didn't even try to keep me up, dropping me in the mud. The action made no sense until suddenly she was behind me and I felt her arms sliding under mine, locking around my chest. When she pulled me around and started dragging me backward, a soft orange glow bloomed across my vision. The heat of it bled into my face, making the stinging worse.

A splash brought contrast to the heat, cold spots spreading along the back of my legs. Natalie kept heaving me, the cold crawling up to consume my legs, my waist, my chest. She didn't stop until it tickled at our chins.

The water seemed glacial after so much heat, knives digging into my skin. Electricity crackled through my right arm, the skin screaming louder there than anywhere else. Natalie was still with me, in front of me now, one arm holding me against her to keep us together.

"Shirt off," I said, hoping to protect Natalie a bit longer.

"What?" she coughed.

"Wet. Over—over heads."

"Right, right."

Thank god she knew me well enough to understand my garbled attempts at speech.

Her hands went to my waist first, despite my attempts to bat them away. When the fabric reached my face, I felt her guide it away from the injury until my shirt was off. Plunging her hands back into the water she took one of mine and guided it until my fingers were twined in one of her belt loops before removing her own shirt. Pushing as close as she could to me, she arranged both shirts over our heads, our noses brushing in the bubble of space. It did seem to provide a bit of relief.

"Where—where's fire?" I managed. I could hear the roar of it, but the distance eluded me.

"It's all around us," Natalie said, arms shaking against my waist.

"Oh."

I wrapped my arms around her as well, unsure what else to do. There was nowhere else to run. Nothing to shield us other than the water and our measly shirts. No way to call for help. Our phones still wouldn't have had signal even if we'd tried, and now they were drowning in our pockets.

The noise of the fire was something else. Was it actually that loud, or were my other senses compensating for my lack of vision? I'd always heard that wildfires sounded like freight trains, but that wasn't what this sounded like. It was a medley of noises; gunshots and engines and wind and car crashes and breaking bones, all layered together, pounding against my skull.

My body was going numb, sensation slipping away from my fingers and toes, receding up my limbs. Except for my face. It still stung. I kind of wished it would go numb too.

"Natalie...."

"Yeah?"

"What's wrong with my face?" Look at me go, forming a whole sentence.

Natalie didn't answer.

"Please."

"Don't worry about it right now."

"Please."

"It's, your, it's—" her voice trembled. I told myself it was from the cold, because that was less terrifying. We could handle cold for a while. But the truth of my injury? I had no idea if I could handle that. "Something burned you. Really bad. It's across both your eyes, but I think the right one is worse. It goes across some of the left side of your forehead and part of your right cheek too."

"Oh." That made sense. Third-degree burns destroyed nerve endings. That's why it felt like there was a hole there.

"It'll be okay," she said, hugging me tighter.

An image floated up in my mind. The last thing I'd seen; a pine tree with fire swallowing up its trunk leaving the outer branches untouched. What a crappy last thing to see. I wished it had been Natalie's face, her smile. Except she wouldn't have been smiling. She would've been terrified. Maybe the tree was better. The only memories I had of what Natalie looked like would be good ones. Her lazing in the hammock in my backyard. Her pouting over a recipe that she couldn't make behave right at our altitude. Her excitement as she talked about what colleges she wanted to go to. Yeah. I'd rather just have those.

Sensation continued to slip away up my limbs as my body gave in to the cold. Neither of us were shaking anymore. That was a bad sign.

The shirts were already mostly dry. Natalie dipped each into the water once more. Even without my eyes, I could tell her movements were disjointed, could feel her struggling to redrape the shirts over us.

It seemed like it was getting harder to breathe too. At first I thought it must be the cold, or the leftover exertion, or the pain. Natalie was gasping , her chest heaving where it was pressed to mine, breaths puffing against my own mouth, and my breathing wasn't any better.

Oxygen. We were running out of oxygen. The fire was swallowing it all up.

"Amazing—how many—ways there are—to die—in a fire,"

I said, struggling to form the words.

Natalie's responding laugh had an edge of delirium. "So many. Burning. Suffocating. Hypothermia. Hyperthermia. Drowning."

"Drowning's supposed—to be nice." I read that somewhere once. That it sucked at first but eventually you just drifted off into a comfortable nothingness. This seemed like a good place for it. Slip down under the water, tangle my arms in the plants so I couldn't come back up. Hide from the pain. Go to sleep, cradled by the mountains I'd been born into.

"I don't want to die," Natalie said, voice now full of tears. "I don't want you to die. I don't want any of us to die."

"I know," I told her, bringing a hand up to caress her cheek, struggling to find it at first. Once I did I ran my thumb along where I knew her freckles were. I should've counted them.

"I love you," she choked out, leaning into the touch.

Following her breath, I pressed my lips to hers. "I love you too."

CHAPTER 13: OUTCROPPING

Dante

Voices floated through my head as I wandered back into the trees. My coach, snapping at me to run another drill, that practice wasn't over yet. My dad, glowing with pride as he told all his friends about my plans to become a smokejumper. Iris, telling me she loved me. My mother, telling me it was okay to rest. Mom was the clearest, the others dipping in and out.

Any awareness of the pain, the heat, was gone. So was most knowledge of what I was doing. Walking? Maybe? Yeah, walking. Walking where? The ground was evening out, which meant...something.

A sticking sensation under my foot brought my attention down and I examined my boot. Brown leather, sooty black now. Black laces. Melted laces. Tiny tendrils of fire kissed at it. I was standing on a rock, though. The flames only had a thin layer of pine needles to fuel them. Attempting to lift my foot again, I realized what the sticking had been. My soles were melting, as was the glue holding them on.

That was it for running, then. Probably walking too.

Oh well.

Rolling my head back upright, I looked around, deciding if this was where I wanted to die. It had probably been pretty once. A thin patch in the trees that was keeping the fire back somewhat. Once the smoke cleared I'd even be under the stars. Stars were nice. Natalie told me once that, on rare occasions, there were even auroras this far south. I'd like to see auroras. Now, though, the area was the center of an inferno. There were no ribbons of green and blue. The opposite, in fact. Ribbons of red and orange.

Maybe the auroras would come later. I just had to lie down and wait for them.

Wind shoved at my back, strong enough to send me stumbling forward until I fell, knees cracking against the ground. Dazed, it took me a moment to realize the change that had occurred. The ground in front of me was no longer on fire. It was just. Rock. Rock continuing out into the distance, obscured by smoke. And it was cool under my fingers. Cooler than the air, anyway.

"Get going, Kristofferson, we're still drilling," Coach snapped. "Come on, up!"

Up wasn't happening. Not all the way.

"Crawl then," Coach answered.

Okay. Yeah. I could crawl.

Feeling like a badly programed robot, I arranged my limbs under me one by one. Right hand first, good. Left hand now, alright. Right leg, got it. Left leg, there we go.

"Get moving. Hurry up."

Progress came one complicated movement at a time. The rock never raised up or dipped down, remaining a flat expanse under me. It never turned back into forest either, taking me farther and farther from the fire as I went. Then, all at once, it fell away and revealed the rest of the world. The drop down was twenty feet onto jagged boulders. A huge swath of the gully was visible beyond that, fire consuming all of it, undulating like waves on the ocean.

There was even a little pond, and...oh...there were people in it. I couldn't see them well, my eyes still blurred with smoke and caked with ash, but they were there. Maybe it was River and Natalie. That would be good. The pond might keep them safe until the fire burned over.

Unsure what else to do, my coach having gone silent, I let myself lay down, looking out over everything. This could've been my job. Jumping into fires like this, being the first man on the ground along with my team. Marching through the trees, chainsaw bobbing on my shoulder, cutting lines to steer the fire, to protect people. We would've made it safe for more teams to follow, got the fire ready for them, held it steady until they found a way in. We'd come out soot-black down to our teeth, pick up a state pin at the local gas station, then wait for the next fire, clinking beers for a job well done.

My team would've had a lookout, someone on an outcropping just like this maybe. A weather kit and good walkie on their belt, calling out the wind and movement of the fire. We would've had a map, safe spots and evac routes. They would watch my back for falling snags from dangerous trees, and I would watch theirs too. We would've had fire shelters to deploy, to hide under and protect us from the heat.

But most of all, we wouldn't have started the fire.

Yes, firefighters did controlled burns, lit backfires. But not in conditions like this. Never in conditions like this.

My mind wandered back to when the fire started, though I had no idea how long that had been. What could I have done differently? How could I have stopped it? More water would've helped. An extinguisher. A phone signal. Anticipating how much of an idiot Toby was. Maybe that wasn't fair, though. I'd really thought that, between me and River, we'd gotten through to him that a campfire was a bad idea.

We never should have brought him.

Why had we brought him?

The wind wouldn't let up, battering me from every angle. I could no longer tell if it was weather wind or fire wind. Sparks sprayed up, like foam from the sea, when a gust crashed a whip of flame against the rocks below me.

It occurred to me that my head was a little clearer now. I was starting to feel things again, including the stinging in my arms. Rolling onto my back, I held them up and examined my skin. The warm brown, darker in the firelight, was glossy pink and white in places. I'd sacrificed the meager protection my flannel gave my arms and used it for my face instead, and this was the consequence. There was blood on my hands as well, dripping down along my arms in sluggish drops. A painful spasm sent my arms curling back against my body, forcing me to suck a breath in through my teeth at the familiar sensation. I'd had dehydration cramps before, gotten so caught up in a game or practice that I didn't drink as much water as I should. But this, this one hurt a thousand times worse.

Once more, I was in a place with less fire and more oxygen, I realized. That's why I was feeling things again. Why my thoughts were getting clearer, just like when I'd fallen on the road. The outcropping was providing enough respite for everything else to catch up to me. Burns, dehydration, smoke inhalation, cuts. Awareness of one tipped into awareness of another and another until all I could do was heave dry sobs, curling in on myself. No longer was my death going to be a quick slide into unconsciousness, my mind gone long before my body caught up and felt what was happening. Now it was going to be agonizing. Slow.

From my curled position on the rapidly warming rock I could still see a sliver of the ground far below me, the jagged boulders there. It wouldn't take much to just...fall. If I went headfirst that would be quick. A new jolt of pain curled me up tighter, knees pulled to my chest, before I could decide. When I managed to look out again, I was greeted by two white eyes.

No, that wasn't right. They were...headlights? Headlights coming down the next ridge, from the direction of the mine. Was it firefighters? It couldn't be. They wouldn't drive in like that, heading down into a fire that was racing uphill. But who else *could* it be?

The lights didn't stop when they reached the edge of the flames, and I lost them among the orange. If it was firefighters, no matter how slim the chance, I had to find a way to signal them. Moving slowly, hoping my arm wouldn't cramp again, I pulled it around until I found my back pocket, felt the familiar rectangle of my phone where I'd tucked it before going after River and Natalie. Digging my fingers in at the bottom of the phone, I pushed it up until it was halfway out, then grabbed it and pulled it around. There wouldn't be signal, but the flashlight might work to get someone's attention.

I pressed the button on the side. Nothing happened. I pressed it a little longer. Nothing happened.

"Oh," I realized. The thing was cooked. My plastic case had warped, bits of what had once been my credit cards oozing out of the back. It was amazing the battery hadn't exploded.

Guess I wouldn't be signaling anyone.

Setting it down on the rock, I let my eyes drift again, watching the flames. The way the fire was moving, it was clear the wind was twisting it in all sorts of directions as it bashed into obstacles. Fire whirls swirled up into the sky and waves rolled through the whole inferno with every change in the wind.

A few times, I thought I saw the headlights again, appearing between breaks in the chaos. What were the odds they were even real? Not great, honestly. There was more oxygen out here, but not as much as I really needed.

They were something to watch, though. Something to keep me from falling over the edge. Maybe I could make it until the fire burned over if I kept focusing. If I could do that...maybe I'd live. I wanted that, I realized. I wanted it desperately.

So I kept watching the lights, making up stories about them. A rogue firefighter determined to perform a rescue. An impossibly stupid tourist. Bigfoot with a flashlight. Anything. Everything. Even my dad, somehow arriving in our beat-up Chevy Blazer. Nothing could kill that thing. Many potholes, deer, and other drivers had tried and failed. It'd survive a fire.

It took me a minute to realize the lights had stopped moving. Flames roiled in front of them, bringing them in and out of view and messing with my perception of where they were, but I was sure they were no longer in motion. Without warning, a boom, barely audible over the fire itself, rang out and an explosion plumed from where the lights had been. The cloud of brighter, yellower flames and heat billowed upwards, rolling in on itself, followed by a column of smoke many shades darker than the smoke coming from the forest.

The headlights were gone.

The fire was still all around me.

I had nothing to distract myself anymore.

Another dry sob bubbled up my throat, stinging the whole way.

"Jesus, take them home," I prayed for the driver and anyone else that had been in the car, if it had even been real, curling back in on myself so I didn't have to watch anymore. I wasn't even sure I believed in Jesus. Right now I didn't care. "Jesus... take me home."

911 Dispatch: Troublesome county 911, do you need police, fire, or EMS?

Caller: I don't know where we are! My wife and I left our AirBNB but we got turned around in the smoke, I don't know where we are!

911 Dispatch: Okay sir, are you going uphill or down?

Caller: Up. Uphill.

911 Dispatch: Okay, I need you to turn around as safely as you can, alright? Whatever county road you're on in that area, going downhill will bring you to the highway. Once you reach it, turn west.

Caller: Which way is west?

911 Dispatch: The fire is coming towards you?

Caller: Yes, and it's so fast.

911 Dispatch: Okay, I know this feels wrong, but once you reach the highway turn towards the direction the fire has been coming from. I think it'll be a right based on what you've told me. Our crews just reached the area and they said the fire hasn't crossed the highway yet. You should be safe to go that way and the firefighters can direct you out once you reach them.

Caller: Okay, okay, we've turned around.

911 Dispatch: Good, go down until you reach the highway, then turn right. When you see emergency vehicles honk your horn and flash your lights. I have to let you go to help other callers.

Caller: Thank you.

@PostUpYourHorses
Just in case before the internet goes:
House 215 in Miner's Village:
People on property: 2 adult males. Lance Mackrel, 24. My brother, Alex, 27.
Bury us back home in Alberta. Tell our parents we're sorry we didn't evacuate. Give my daughter a kiss. #LostHenFire
↻304 | ❤1,282

Engine 41: 41 ETA five minutes. There's a caravan of evacuees coming towards us, but we can't stop to direct them.

Captain Henderson: Can you see the fire?

Engine 41: Hang on, coming around the last bend now.

Engine 41: Hell, this baby's roaring.

Captain Henderson: Can you see any way to work it?

Engine 41: No sir. It's already at the Village. We're going in for evac. Someone link up with the caravan and try and figure out who we still need to find.

Officer Turner: Engine 41, Officer Turner. I'll get them, I'm only a few minutes behind you.

Engine 41: Copy that. Cap, can you confirm one of the missing kids is Dante? The one who volunteers with us?

Captain Henderson: Yeah, it is. Keep your heads. I know we all care about him but we can't be stupid, understood?

Engine 41: Yes sir.

CHAPTER 14: COP

Emmy kept her hand pressed to her mouth, tears rolling silently down her face from tightly closed eyes. No one said a word. My ears continued to ring from the roar of the fire, even though it wasn't audible anymore. Dante was still up there. River was still up there. Natalie was still up there. It hadn't even been two hours since we'd arrived at the campsite. It wasn't even fully dark yet. How had so much happened in so little time?

The only thing that kept me going forward instead of turning around were the other people in the truck.

"Iris?" a soft voice said from behind my seat.

"Yeah, Clark?" I asked, my voice unsteady.

"Do you think our horses will be okay?"

I sniffed. "Yeah, yeah I think they'll be alright. Horses are really smart, they'll run to safety. And you put your number on them."

"We won't have anywhere to put them, though."

Emmy's tears started coming faster, her shoulders shaking.

"You can keep them at my place," I said. We only had three stalls, two of them in use, but I didn't care. We'd figure it out.

"Thanks."

She fell silent and I rubbed my face on my shoulder to get rid of some of my own tears. Twelve years old and she was losing everything.

"We'll get through this," Mable said. "These mountains have burned before. It will be alright."

No one answered her. Sure, they had burned before. Plenty of times. But not like this.

When the hillside ahead of us lit up red, I almost screamed, thinking that somehow there was another fire. That we'd gotten turned around. That the fire had changed directions. Before my panic turned into real action, a fire truck careened around the curve, sirens blaring and lights blazing. Another was close behind, and a third, plus a few police cars. The caravan all pulled over, giving them as much room as absolutely possible. People in truck beds all down the line stood up, cheering and waving as the firefighters went, sending a fresh wave of pain through my chest. Those people thought the firefighters would be able to save their homes. They didn't realize there wasn't time. A glance back showed Toby hunched down, biting his lip.

Another siren rang out, this time the source revealing itself as a single cop car. It stopped at the front of the caravan and an officer got out. He was a statey, though, not a local cop, so I didn't recognize him. The local department was contracted with my dad's mechanic shop for repairs, but the stateys went somewhere else.

The officer motioned to the whole line to stay put, then went up to the first vehicle, flipped open a notepad, and spoke to the people inside. After jotting a few things down, he waved them on, then repeated it with the next truck. Two more and he'd be at my window.

Looking at Toby again I saw him watching the cop with wide eyes that darted to the fields off to the side of the road several times.

Oh hell no.

I shut the engine off, handing the keys over to Emmy. She took them, looking at me in confusion.

"This truck belongs to River Ashworth. Her family lives at 868 Falcon Way. If you see them before I do, tell them...tell them...their daughter is missing in the fire," I told her.

"I don't understand what's happening," Emmy said, keys dangling from her hand.

Taking a deep breath, I met her gaze as steadily as I could. "Don't look out the back window. The boy I'm with? He's the one who started the fire. We tried to stop him, but he wouldn't listen. I think he's planning to get out and run."

Emmy's eyes widened and I could see her fighting the urge to look.

"I'm going to make sure he doesn't, and that he pays for this, I promise," I told her. "Promise me you'll get the truck back to River's parents."

Emmy held the keys to her chest and nodded.

"Iris?" Clark said, poking her head up between the front seats.

"Yeah?"

"Punch him for me."

This startled a laugh out of me. "Sorry, I'm rubbish at punching. Broke my thumb once."

"I'm not," Mable chirped.

I chuckled. "He's all yours then."

Turning, I opened the door and stepped out, dirt and gravel crunching under my feet. The cop, only one car ahead now, instantly turned his attention to me. Ignoring him, I marched back to stand across from Toby. He was lit in stark shadows by the headlights of the truck behind us, the lighting throwing his panic into sharp relief.

"Get out," I ordered.

The other people around him looked between Toby and me, clearly confused.

Toby shrunk back. "Why?"

"Get out."

Toby shook his head. "I'm good here."

"Get out."

"What's going on over here?" The cop asked, appearing at my shoulder, also glancing back and forth at Toby and me. The person driving the truck behind us was leaning out the window to listen.

"Nothing," Toby said before I could speak. He couldn't have sounded guiltier if he'd tried.

The officer raised an eyebrow, posture tensing slightly. "Look, my name's Officer Turner, alright? I'm just here to make a list of who got out of the Village."

"Understandable," I said. "And we'll let you get back to it as soon as Toby tells you what he needs to."

"I don't need to tell him anything!" Toby said, voice loud enough to start drawing more attention from the other vehicles.

Officer Turner's hand twitched towards his taser.

"If you don't tell him the truth, Toby, I will," I said, no real hope that he'd listen behind my words.

Toby looked at me with begging eyes. "The fire—well— we were camping—and the firepit, I think someone else was there first because it just sort of went up." His eyes were still desperate, willing me to back him up. He couldn't have looked more pathetic if he tried, all curled shoulders and trembling lip. It was such a picture-perfect expression of the emotion I knew it had to be fake. Just another practiced tantrum that always got him what he wanted when he did it with everyone else. I wondered if this was how he reacted when he wrecked his Jeep, if we'd ever heard the real story behind that accident. He said he'd swerved to avoid an elk, but now I couldn't help but wonder if there was any truth in that at all.

"Try again," I responded. "Last chance, Toby."

He shook his head. "That's what happened. That's what happened!"

Everyone listening was looking at him with suspicion now. Even the two dogs were picking up on the tension, whining and fidgeting. Clark and Emmy were staring from inside the cab.

"You're such a coward," I said, trying to figure out what to do. What I was willing to do. What the others would want me to do.

Natalie probably would have protected him. I didn't think she'd back up his lie, but she would have found a way to soften the truth somehow. She loved him too much to do anything else, even if that love came from a bad place of always having to look out for him and clean up after him ever since they were kids, and never having reason to question that. River had been growing noticeably more exasperated with Toby over the summer, so I doubted she'd protect him. And Dante may have tried to help him out of a lot of other things, at least somewhat, but not this. Not for a fire.

I turned to face Officer Turner. "This is Tobias Cassidy. We were camping with three other friends and, despite us telling him not to and trying to stop him, he lit a campfire. The pit was stone-cold before what he did. We tried to put it out but the wind picked up and within minutes it was too late. Our other three friends are missing in the fire."

"No! No I didn't! I didn't do it!" Toby wailed.

"What are these friends' names?" The cop asked, ignoring Toby for the moment.

"River Ashworth, Dante Kristofferson, and Natalie McLain," I told him. "Also, another guy, Adam Delgado, came up in a water truck from the mine. He's out there looking for the others."

"Okay, and your name?"

"Iris Sawyer."

Toby began to gasp and hiccup as if he were sobbing, yet not a single tear made it out of his eyes. Everyone had moved away from him, and no one looked convinced by the act.

"Alright, Iris, we were already aware of the five of you being out there. I will radio in that two of you are accounted for, but for now all of you need to continue on out of the area. An evacuation center is being set up at the high school."

"All of us?" I said, glancing at Toby.

Three more fire trucks roared by, forcing the cop to pause before he answered. "Yes, all of you."

"Hell no, I ain't riding to town with the kid who just burned down my home!" a man snapped.

I swallowed heavily. It was one thing to tell the truth of what happened and then let the officer take it from there. But if I kept pushing, a lot more of the weight of Toby's arrest—and hopefully his eventual consequences—would rest on my shoulders. But if I didn't, the weight of not doing so would be just as heavy. Maybe heavier. "Officer Turner, sir, that is not a good idea," I insisted. "Toby's family is extremely wealthy and they have homes in three countries. He has never faced a consequence in his life because his parents always prevented it. If you do not arrest him now, if you allow him to get back to his parents first, you will never see him again, and I'm not going to let that happen." What kept my voice steady I couldn't say. Maybe it was the desperation to feel like I was accomplishing something amidst all of this. Toby had to face consequences.

"It's not my fault!" Toby insisted, still not really crying but trying to act like it. "You can't arrest me! It's not my fault!"

"Officer, either take this kid or give me your cuffs and we'll drop him off at the station on our way in," the man with the toddler on his lap said.

Officer Turner debated for a moment longer, then nodded, motioning for Toby to get out. Toby shrunk back, shaking his head over and over.

"It wasn't my fault! It wasn't my fault!"

The man with the toddler handed the child off to the woman next to him, then crouched next to Toby. "Son, you are going to get out of this truck willingly or this fine officer and I are going to remove you by force."

"Let's go," Officer Turner said.

Toby looked between them a couple times, then slowly stood up, body starting to shake in a much less intentional way. Clinging to the edge of the bed, he swung one leg over and placed his foot on the tire before swinging his other leg over as well. I wanted to feel vindication, revel in the fact that he was realizing what his actions had caused. Except I knew he didn't care about any of that. Not our missing friends. Not the people still in the Village. Not the people who had lost everything. He only cared that he'd been caught.

"It wasn't my fault," he whimpered once more.

"Turn around," the officer instructed. "Hands on the back of your head. Is there anything on your person that could stick or harm me in any way?"

"N—no," Toby stammered, doing as told.

By now people had gotten out of the cars behind us, watching and whispering. Turning meant Toby was facing all of them, brightly lit in the headlights. Four more cop cars, another firetruck, and an ambulance came by as Toby was read his rights, hands cuffed behind his back one by one.

"Look at them. They lost everything because of you," I told him, tears starting to roll down my face. "Their homes, their pets, every scrap of memory hung on their walls and stored on their shelves. It's all ash because of you." Even if he didn't care, I needed to say it. Needed him to hear it.

The cop took him on the long walk back to the squad car, putting Toby in the back, and only realized I'd followed when he turned around.

"Miss, please get back in your truck," he asked.

I shook my head. "I'm getting in yours."

"Miss—"

"Until I know what happened to my friends, I'm staying here. Arrest me if you have to, I was there too, after all."

He sighed, gesturing to the passenger seat. "You're not under arrest, but I don't have time for this argument. Get in and do not touch anything. I will be back once I check the rest of the caravan and radio numbers and names to everyone else."

"Thank you," I said, sliding into the SUV.

He walked away before the door was closed.

"Iris, what the fuck?" Toby said from behind me. "Why did you tell him it was my fault? It was so dry up there, anything could have started a fire!"

"You're right, anything could have. Which is why you *shouldn't* have. Now shut up. I'm not doing this anymore," I told him, slumping against the leather and resting my forehead on the cool glass of the window. "It was your fault. People are dead because of you, maybe even our friends. Just be quiet."

"Iris—"

"Quiet."

He sniffed and I heard the seat groan as he leaned back.

River's truck rumbled by, Emmy looking out at us from the driver's seat. I couldn't meet her eyes.

The huge radio in the dash spilled out sickening words, sentence after sentence outlining exactly what was going on with just enough detail to not be quite enough.

"We have three houses burning and multiple smaller structures."

"One elderly man refusing to evacuate. He's in a bulldozer, trying to cut line. Fire's already on him."

"Potential fatality found, attempting resuscitation in the truck."

"This is 41, no sign of anyone yet. Continuing up 32."

"Another holdout. He's on his porch drinking whiskey. Has a shotgun next to him but is not holding it."

"We went through and evacuated everyone we could. If they're choosing to stay there, that's...they're choosing to stay there."

"You've done what you can. Document holdouts and move on. This fire's going too hard to linger."

"She's about to jump the highway near the Village. Spraying things down now."

"Don't stay if you don't have somewhere to shelter up, if she jumps she jumps."

Even the firm, trained tone of everyone's voices couldn't mask the sense of chaos. Unable to take it anymore, and ignoring the instruction not to touch anything, I searched until I found a volume dial, using it to mute the radio. Pulling my knees up to my chest and wrapping my arms around them, I dropped my head and gave in to the fear and panic at last.

911 Dispatch: Troublesome County 911, do—

Caller: HELP! MY HOUSE IS ON FIRE! I'M IN THE VILLAGE! OH GOD, HELP!

911 Dispatch: Are you inside your house or out—

Caller: HELP ME!

911 Dispatch: Ma'am, I need you to stop screaming. Are you inside or outside?

Caller: Why didn't they warn us? Why didn't they warn us? Please, help me.

911 Dispatch: *Are you inside or outside your home?*

Caller: Out—outside.

911 Dispatch: Get in your car and leave immediately.

Caller: I can't, it's in the garage! It's on fire! Why aren't you helping me?

911 Dispatch: I am doing everything I can. If you cannot get to your car you need to go on foot. Head for the highway.

Caller: Help me, help me. Oh god, why hasn't it rained? Please help me.

911 Dispatch: Ma'am, run. Run now.

911 Dispatch: Ma'am? Hello?

911 Dispatch: Hello?

911 Dispatch: Hello?

Engine 41: We've passed the Village, it's all lost. We're heading up Dirty Bird to find the kids. 46 and 48 are staying to help the Village.

Elliot: No, stay on 32 until it ends. One of my guys is already on Dirty Bird searching, the other was coming down over Gulch Road. Cover ground they haven't.

Engine 41: Got it. Vehicle descriptions?

Elliot: 1990s Ford Pumper Tankers, big red ones with the decals stripped.

Engine 41: Copy.

Engine 62: Anyone else see that plume of dark black smoke that just started up?

Elliot: Where?

Engine 62: North of the Village, bit to the east.

Elliot: There's nothing up there that would burn black like that.

Engine 62: Could be a car, maybe?

Elliot: ….

Captain Henderson: Elliot? Did you copy?

Elliot: That's…that's the way one of my guys went. Shawn. Dante's dad.

Captain Henderson: Dammit.

Engine 41: 41 here, should we divert to it?

Captain Henderson: …no. If it is, was, a vehicle explosion there won't be survivors to find. Keep looking for the kids. They may still have a chance, if they found a safe place to hole up. We know Dante at least knows what to do.

Elliot: Shawn went out to rescue Dante, he'd want you to find his son. Keep looking for Dante.

Engine 41: Understood.

CHAPTER 15: RUN FOR IT

Adam

My eyes stung from being outside in the smoke and ash even for such a short time. What this must be like for anyone stuck out here, I didn't want to consider. They were exposed to everything. I'd driven through the flames, yeah, but the keyword there was *driven*. Not run on foot.

It was only moments before I was out of the black, burned over area, diving back into rising flames. They started small, dancing only a few feet off the ground, emanating from the last bits of unburned fuel. Little by little they rose up, closed back in around me, painted everything hazy orange. The heat leached in through the windows, making me sweat. I wanted to find something to wipe it away, but the hand that wasn't gripping the wheel was slamming down on the horn when I didn't need to shift. As brutal as the roar of the flames was, I hoped the horn could cut through enough to lead anyone to me.

Driving as slowly as I dared, I scanned my gaze across the flickering landscape, struggling to focus through the layers and layers of flame. I looked between each pillar of fire climbing up the trees, stared into thickets hoping to see someone dashing towards me, constantly checked my mirrors for anyone behind. Nothing. The closest thing I saw to a sign of life was several dead elk lying in the road. Without a better option, I ran them over, glad I couldn't hear the sound of it.

A few new warning lights had flickered to life on the dash, and I was sure if I could distinguish the sound of the engine, it wouldn't sound great. Unable to do anything other than continue forward, I didn't let myself look too closely at the lights. Thinking about what would happen if the truck died was also not an option.

I was nearly in the bottom of the gully now, still no sign of any of the three people I was after. Nor, for that matter, Shawn. Depending on how long he'd had to stop to help the family of campers, this should've been almost where we'd cross paths unless he'd managed to come out ahead of me and turned South on 32 to head towards the Village. I couldn't fathom him doing that, though. Not without his son. An uneasy feeling settled in my gut, but I didn't even bother to try the radio. I hadn't heard a word over it since I'd left the campsite. Maybe the signal was blocked. Maybe the fire was interfering somehow. Maybe the antenna had melted off. No matter the reason, I was alone out here right now.

Turning around the last bend before the bottom, the fire began to lay down, now only fueled by the short, scrubby sage as the towering pines thinned out. My gaze swept across the landscape, aching eyes hungry for anything other than fire. There was nothing *but* fire, though, and a wind-churned expanse of water: Upper Pond. It was half empty from the drought, surrounded by a cracked expanse of dried mud, chaotic waves lapping at its shores. The tumultuous black water reflected a fractured kaleidoscope of the fire. The pond itself would've been hard to distinguish if not for the ring of unburning mud surrounding it.

The way the water made the fire flicker and change in that little area seemed to make my eyes ache more than the fire itself, a headache building behind them. Unable to fight the urge to blink, I almost missed the frantically waving arm rising out of the pond. Slamming on the brakes, I looked closer, hoping what I'd seen was real, not some trick of the light making a stick look like an arm.

It wasn't. In the center of the pond and coming closer were two people, one dragging the other. I realized, though, that once they got out of the water and mud they'd have twenty yards of fire to go through to get to me.

I'd stolen this truck for a moment exactly like this, a moment where there would be a sprawling line of fire in the way of someone getting to safety. Yet the only way to do anything about it was to get out, to go into the fire, and that was a much more daunting task now that I was on the brink of doing it.

They needed me, though. Time to make this truck earn its death.

Throwing the door open, I jumped out, feet slamming into the gravel of the road. Wind ripped and tore at my clothes, throwing embers and sparks along with it. Outside the protection of the truck, the heat in the heart of the fire was beyond anything I could've imagined. My body wanted to curl up, hide from the searing ache, instinct telling me to get away get away get away, get back in the truck.

It was a fight just to make it to the back where the hose had been rigged to spray the roads. Like many companies, the one that owned the mine hadn't been willing to buy us the expensive good equipment. This truck wasn't made to wet down roads, it was made to fight fires, so we'd had to jury-rig up a system that worked with what we had. Now I had to unjury-rig it, and quickly. A short fire hose came from the main valve of the water tank and coiled around the end of it twice before the nozzle draped down to sit on the bumper, pointing backward. It was all held in place with a mixture of zip-ties, duct tape, and wire. A few colorful blobs dripping down the hose marked where the zip-ties had once been. This left only the wires, and a quick twist of the one holding the nozzle to the bumper freed roughly ten feet of hose, the wire still dangling from the handle. That was enough.

I almost reached for the nozzle of the hose without thinking, barely stopping in time. Grabbing it outright would probably be bad. Pulling my hardhat off with one hand, I yanked off my top-most long-sleeved shirt with the other, leaving me in only a tank top. I put the hardhat back on and draped the long-sleeved shirt around the nozzle hauling it up and dragging it with me to the exterior controls. With my shirt already in use, there was nothing to protect my fingers from the latch on the little door. Gritting my teeth I tugged it open as quick as I could, feeling my flesh cook in just that single moment. Relief flooded through me at the sight of a bit of tape next to a set of dials, the words "hose control" written on it. There was one switch and one dial, both almost as hot as the latch, burning me again as I started up the hose. Not wanting to drain the water too quickly, I kept the pressure low.

I thought about dousing myself first, desperate for the cool water, but I realized it would just risk dangerous steam burns so I turned the hose towards the sage, trying to cut a path for the people in the pond. They'd reached the edge of it, one hanging off the side of the other, unable to stand. When the water hit the flames it vaporized, great clouds of steam billowing up and obscuring any view I had of the people. I didn't let up, though, letting the hose rise and fall to, hopefully, tamp the fire down enough for them to make a dash for the truck. What little I could see showed that maybe it was working.

Then they were there, soaking wet and stumbling. Their faces were wrapped in wet shirts, leaving them in only bras and pants, and their shoes were in pieces. Keeping the hose in one hand I went for them, scooping up the other side of the stumbling person to get them to the truck faster. The other girl and I shoved the stumbling one up through the driver's door, and she scrambled in after. With them inside I threaded the still spraying hose through the bracket of the side mirror, draped it up on the hood, and twisted the wire around the support of one of the wiper blades so the hose sprayed out over the hood of the truck and a bit out in front. Slipping under it I made it back into the cab, slamming the door.

"River! River!" The seemingly less injured girl said, panic lacing every word.

The stumbling girl was unconscious, sprawled out across the middle and passenger portions of the bench seat, her head lolling in the other girl's lap.

River. Okay, so that meant the other girl must be: "Natalie."

She was rocking, one hand cradling River's chin, the other stroking her hair, and didn't answer.

"Natalie!" I shouted. "Are you Natalie?"

She nodded.

"Where is Dante?" I asked.

She shook her head, answering in a voice that seemed to cause her pain to use, "We got separated. We got separated."

Damn.

There was no time left to look for him, though. Not with River in the condition she was.

As soon as the truck was in gear and moving forward I pulled the mic of the radio off the dash again, unsure if it would do any good. I had to try, though. "This is Adam Delgado, I have River and Natalie in my truck. No sign of Dante. River is unconscious and needs immediate medical attention. Does anyone copy?"

"This is Engine 41, we copy. Can you make it out?"

"We're about to find out," I answered.

"What's your location?"

"Just south of Upper Pond, heading south on 32."

"Understood. Is there any update on Dante's last known location?"

"Hang on."

I looked at Natalie. She'd turned on the overhead light and removed the shirt around River's head, giving me a real look at River's face. I flinched at the sight of her exposed features, haloed by sooty blond hair. Everything around her eyes was burned, badly, skin raw and peeling, twisted and mangled. Natalie was gently stroking River's unburned chin, talking to her so softly I couldn't hear.

"Natalie," I said, getting her attention. "Where did you last see Dante?"

She blinked a few times, shirt removed from her own head as well. I could see the effort it was taking her to string her thoughts together and realized she may not have a burned face, but she wasn't much better off than River.

I repeated the question, slower.

"Half—halfway down the hill," Natalie managed. Her voice was sandpaper, almost inaudible. "He had to go right, I think. South. He got pushed south."

I passed the information on.

"Understood, we're coming north up 32 now," 41 responded. "Get those two out and leave Dante to us."

"Understood," I told them before hanging the mic back up.

When I shifted the truck into the next gear, it felt wrong. Rougher. Maybe it was because my hand was burned, screaming as it wrapped around the eight ball.

"Go faster," Natalie pleaded.

Gritting my teeth against the pain in my hand, I shifted up one more gear. There was definitely something wrong with the transmission.

A lot more warning lights were on the dash now. This was turning into a very uncomfortable balancing act of getting out quick and not blowing the engine.

"Hang on to something," I told Natalie. "This'll be rough."

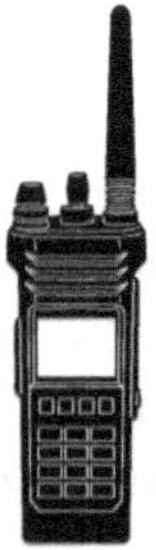

Adam: 41, are you who I just passed?

Engine 41: Yeah that was us.

Adam: Did you see another tender before you passed me?

Engine 41: No, just you. Are you talking about the one with Dante's dad?

Adam: Yeah. He was coming up over Gulch Road. I should've passed him coming out or you should've passed him coming in.

Adam: Hello?

Engine 41: We've already been told to be on the lookout for him. Just keep going and get out of here.

Adam: He won't leave until he finds his son.

Engine 41: Neither will we.

@JessicaLostIt
@TroubleCoFire I found an online broadcast of the local emergency radio chatter for the #LostHenFire. They said there's holdouts. I think one is my dad, in the bulldozer. Please get him, please. I'm begging you. Make him leave!
↻5 | ♥9

Engine 41: We've spotted someone, we think it's Dante. He's on a rock outcropping. Attempting to reach him now.

Captain Henderson: Don't be stupid. I know he's one of ours, but don't be stupid.

CHAPTER 16: ESCAPE

Dante

All my pain slipped away once more. So had sensation in general, actually. No scratching of the rock against my arms. No heat soaking through my skin and down into my bones. No ache in my muscles from dehydration and exertion. Even the orange leaching through my eyelids was fading to black.

There was no tunnel. There were no flashes of memory. How disappointing. I wanted to see Iris one more time. Kiss her one more time. Why couldn't my mind give me that? Let me rewind to earlier, erase Toby, and give me the night with Iris I wanted. That would've been better than this slow slide into nothingness.

I should've let myself fall off the cliff.

I didn't want to be here anymore.

I wanted Iris.

I wanted my Mom.

I wanted to sle—

Lighting shot up my arm, pain exploding back into my awareness. No part of me could comprehend what was happening, only that it buzzed out from something wrapped around my upper arm. The rock vanished from underneath me, my eyes flying open only to see the whole world tilting and spinning. Was I caught in a fire whorl? Had the rock broken away in the heat, sending me tumbling?

I was upside down now, unsure how I got there, hanging awkwardly, only able to see an expanse of brown canvas. Whatever had clamped onto my arm was now around my wrist, which didn't feel any better, and there was something looped around one of my legs as well. I couldn't muster up any energy to fight what was happening. How did my death keep getting worse? Every time the pain vanished something went and brought it back.

Let me go, I thought.

Please let me go.

Why couldn't this be over?

Two more lightning bolts attached themselves to my arms, yanking roughly.

Please stop.

It did stop. Had I managed to ask it out loud? I didn't think I could have.

And was it quieter now? Cooler?

There was still noise, lots of it, and a strange, glowing yellow square floating above me. What was the noise? I knew I recognized it, but couldn't call up its name.

A blurry tan shape blocked out the yellow square, part of it moving.

Face. It was a face.

And the noise was voices.

Hands came up, one sliding under my neck as the other unwound my flannel from around my head. A mask was pressed over my face. Not a medical one, it covered my whole face. I could see out, though.

Cool air rushed into my mouth and nose and I felt my lungs dragging it in, desperate for more, expanding so much it felt like my chest couldn't take it. My hands scrabbled for the mask, trying to press it closer, to get more of the air.

"Easy, easy, Dante," the person above me said, the first clear words that made it all the way into my head. "Slow, deep breaths."

Listening was hard. I needed more. I forced myself to do it, though, inhaling the air in one long pull before letting it slip back out. Again. Again.

"There you go," the person said. "We got you, Dante. Keep taking steady breaths."

My vision began to clear, details of wherever I was fading in out of the haze my mind had been in before. There was a second man, down by my legs, his torso leaned forward between two sets of cabinets. I was on a hard floor, two chairs with folded up seats above me and the handle of an ax next to my face.

Piece by piece it all clicked together. Firetruck. I was in a firetruck. I was alive, and I was in a firetruck.

Natalie. River. Iris.

I had to tell the firefighter.

Why weren't the words coming out?

The firefighter who'd given me the mask wasn't even looking at me now, instead pulling something out of one of the cabinets behind him. His hands reappeared above me, holding an oblong blueish shape.

I had to tell him.

One hand let go of the strange shape, the other tilting it over onto its side. Everything went white, except this time it wasn't pain, it was relief as the water rolled over me. Only desperation to tell him about the others kept me from succumbing to the coolness spreading across my battered skin. It didn't last, though, and the pain surged back worse than before. Something else cool came almost immediately, pushing the pain back down. Reorienting myself I saw the firefighter pulling open some kind of paper package, removing the long strips inside, and laying them along my arms. They felt amazing. Even better than the water.

"Friends," I managed.

He leaned closer. "What?"

"My friends." God, talking hurt. Gargling sand would've been more pleasant.

"Just hang in there a bit longer, Dante, alright, we're gonna get you to an ambulance."

"My friends," I repeated, trying to make myself louder.

He frowned, turning to the other firefighter, whispering to him. The man glanced down at me, then gave a nod and whispered something back.

The first firefighter turned back, hovering over me. "Natalie,

River, Iris, and Toby are all safe."

If I could've cried I would have.

Between the oxygen flowing out of the mask and whatever was on my arms, my awareness continued to trickle back in. The truck was moving roughly underneath me, bouncing and jostling. Padded foil blankets covered the two back windows, an orange glow emanating from around their edges.

"We're not," I realized.

"We almost are," he said.

"Who are you?" I rasped. I felt like I should know him, but my mind wouldn't give me a name.

He frowned, worry etched around his eyes. "It's Peter, we saw each other a few hours ago when you were at the station remember?"

Oh. Right. I'd been volunteering. Scrubbing engines. Sweeping floors. Helping cook lunch. Peter had waved goodbye to me when River picked me up. Had that really been only a few hours ago?

"They hurt?" I asked, hoping he knew what I meant as I rationed my words. The more the pain in my arms faded, the more other pains rose up. A scratching ache in my eyes. Muscles seizing with cramps. Stinging cuts on my hands.

Peter swallowed, looking uncomfortable. "Don't worry about it right now, they're safe, that's what matters."

"Peter," I begged. Not knowing was worse. Not knowing let me imagine things.

Peter had another whispered debate with the other firefighter before he answered me, reluctance in every word. "I think Iris and Toby are fine, but River and Natalie were hurt. Don't know how bad. Someone else found them just before we found you."

That made sense. Iris and Toby had gotten out while River and Natalie had been forced to run.

"Toby did this," I said. It seemed very important that Peter know.

We went over a particularly large bump, my body floating for a second before smacking back down. Peter managed to ride it out better, able to brace himself against the motion.

"It's gonna get worse," a voice from the front of the cab said. "Lotta snags down in the road."

"We're running them?" Peter asked.

"No other option. They're small for now."

Peter dug around in the cabinets again, producing a scratchy gray blanket this time. He tucked it under my head, then placed one hand over my chest, his other hand braced on the back wall.

"Toby started the fire," I said.

The truck slammed over another bump, but Peter's firm hand kept me in place.

"Okay," Peter said. "I hear you, Dante. We'll make sure to pass it on. Just hang in there for me, alright?"

Hanging on didn't seem to matter quite as much anymore. Everyone was safe. They knew Toby had done it. What else was there?

The walls of a well climbed up around the edges of my vision, rising higher and higher, blotting out my vision

"Dante? Hey, Dante, keep your eyes open."

Why?

"Dante? Come on, eyes open."

The walls of the well were getting taller.

"Dante, answer me. Come on."

Iris was safe. Peter knew about Toby.

Soft blackness slipped over my vision, and I didn't fight it.

Engine 41: This is 41, we've recovered Dante. Need medical waiting.

Captain Henderson: Copy. Any sign of the missing tender?

Engine 41: No, and don't radio the driver's name.

Captain Henderson: Dante's conscious?

Engine 41: Somewhat.

Captain Henderson: Understood. ETA?

Engine 41: Fast as we can. Road's getting rough. Had to run some snags. There's nowhere to turn around up here either, we had to keep going up the hill.

Captain Henderson: Understood. You should be in the black soon and able to come down around the back of it.

Engine 41: Copy that.

CHAPTER 17: REUNITED

Iris

What I expected was for Officer Turner to eventually climb back in, turn the terrifying radio back on, call in the notes he'd taken, and turn us around to head back to town. What I got was the sound of rapidly crunching gravel outside the windows, looking up just in time to see him yank the door open, slam inside, and jam his key into the ignition.

"What's happening?" I asked, unsure why I had. I didn't really want to know.

"They need medical help at the Village," was all the officer said. He pressed a button on the dash, the siren wailing out. Foot to the floor, he skidded back into motion, heading in the direction of the fire. He didn't bother to turn the volume back up on the radio, but his personal one on his shoulder continued to crackle with calls.

No, no, no. I didn't want to see it again.

"There's already an ambulance," I said. "I saw it go by."

He shot me an apologetic look. "Only one. It isn't enough. I was a paramedic before I took this job. Just curl back up and don't look if you need to."

It was too late, though. Coming around a bend in the road revealed pillars of fire arcing over the highway in the distance. Whatever may have been left of the Village was completely obscured. Official vehicles were knotted together near the turnoff for County Road 32, looking like they were scrambling to pull back.

Toby let out a little noise of shock behind me, starting to mumble "it's not my fault" over and over again.

"How much trouble would I get in if I asked you to turn around and shoot him?" I asked flatly.

"Enough that you're lucky our department can't afford enough body cams for everyone."

"Noted."

Now that I was seeing it, I couldn't look away. Had the flames been this tall the whole time? They seemed taller now, even out in the sage on the south side of the highway. A city skyline of undulating hell.

Officer Turner stopped the SUV a ways back from the others. "Stay here, I'll be back as soon as I can."

With that he jumped out, going around the back and pulling out some sort of medical kit, jogging with it to the other vehicles. There were just as many people in uniform as out. One woman sat on the bumper of a firetruck, badly burned arms held out in front of her as she swayed, a dazed look on her face. A young boy, no more than six, clung to a bright green teddy bear, eyes wide. When a firefighter spotted him standing there alone the firefighter scooped him up and deposited him in the cab of an engine.

Heat from the fire leached into the SUV, even from this far away. My skin ached from it, Dante, River, and Natalie floating to the forefront of my mind again. They'd died in this. Died with their skin screaming, their lungs aching.

"Iris…" Toby whispered from the backseat.

"What?"

"I really didn't mean to do this."

I closed my eyes and took a deep breath, swallowing heavily. "It doesn't matter what you *meant*, Toby, it matters what you *did*. Dante told you not to. River told you not to. The news has told you not to for *months*. But you did it anyway."

"But—"

I spun around to glare at him. "Stop saying 'but'! Stop making excuses! You. Did. This. Look me in the eye and explain what possible logic you're using to think you aren't responsible."

He struggled to hold my gaze, eyes flitting from mine to the fire behind me.

"The wind—"

"The wind didn't start it, Toby. The wind wouldn't have mattered at all if you didn't start it. You made a choice, and this is the consequence. That's it. That's all."

"...do you really think they're dead?" he asked, voice small.

"Do you really think there's a way they wouldn't be?"

Tears started rolling down his face, real ones this time, and he didn't respond.

"This isn't your Jeep, Toby. Your parents can't buy your way out, so you better come to terms with what you've done," I said, turning my back to him once more.

The scene in front of me was as chaotic as it had been before, people dashing all around. Some were firemen, hauling hoses back towards their trucks in preparation to pull out. Others were cops trying to drag reluctant civilians away. There didn't seem to be any order to what was happening. Just scared people doing whatever seemed right in the moment.

As close as the fire had come to the knot of emergency responders and evacuees, the wind so far seemed to be holding it back from coming closer. It rolled the flames back on themselves over and over, layers of red and orange and yellow and white.

Past the turnoff, County Road 32 wasn't on fire itself, but it was not clear of flames. They arced over it, pushed to the ground by the wind. I watched the gap as it came and went, knowing that somewhere on the other side were people I loved. The bodies of people I loved.

When something ballooned out of the base of the fire through the gap I jumped, startled by what seemed like an explosion. It came in a shower of sparks and embers, flames and smoke enveloping it. Only when it reached the edge of the group of other vehicles did I realize it was another firetruck. Had been another firetruck. Even from a distance I could see the paint was bubbled and peeling, the body warped in spots, and the tires had brought the fire with them. Tendrils licked up over the hubs, getting far too close to the engine. A hose hung limply from one of the side mirrors, the dry nozzle pointing over the hood.

The thing was so damaged, I didn't even fully realize what

it was until it skidded to a stop in the middle of everyone else. Adam. It was Adam's truck.

I grabbed at the door handle, tumbling out into the heat and chaos, sprinting the distance between me and whoever was inside that truck. The driver's side door swung open halfway before being stopped by the hose, forcing Adam to slide out under it, the hose catching on his hardhat and sending it tumbling to the ground. Fire from the tires kissed his heavy jeans and bare arms as he dashed around the hood to the passenger door, but he didn't seem to notice.

There was someone else in there, I could see their outline now. But...who? There was soot on the windshield, obscuring details. A head of frizzy brown hair came into view through the muck as I got closer. Natalie. Was it just Natalie?

Please don't just be Natalie. Please let the others be there too.

I stopped a few feet away, terrified of what I might see but desperate to know.

Adam pulled open the passenger door and leaned into the cab, one foot up on the step and a firefighter coming up behind him. Together they pulled out a limp body that flopped into their arms. The firefighter's shoulders blocked my view of everything except a tumble of singed blond hair.

River.

That just left....

Natalie nearly fell out of the truck after River, wearing only her pants and a bra, desperately clinging to River's foot and crying so hard she wasn't making a sound. I needed to follow. To find out what was wrong with River. But I needed to know. Dante. I needed to know.

I didn't want to know.

I wanted to go back to last week, when he'd showed up at the barn with a meatball sandwich from Subway—the only fast food for an hour in any direction—to surprise me, bringing a bag of Fiddle's favorite treats as well.

I wanted to go back to when he'd first asked me out, stumbling and awkward and patient enough to wait for me to figure out if I trusted his interest or not.

I wanted to go back to the first time I fell asleep curled up against him, to how cozy and safe that had felt.

I didn't want to know.

I needed to know.

As the firefighter carried River away I stepped around to look into the cab.

It was empty.

Nothing except a little tire gauge on the floor.

"No." I whimpered.

A hand landed softly on my shoulder and I turned to see Adam standing there, his other hand cradled to his chest, the palm of it shiny pink. He was only in a soot-stained white tank top, the long-sleeved gray shirt he'd had on before now gone. His face was black with soot as well, rivulets of sweat carving out stripes of his real skin.

"Natalie says they got split up. A crew is still out there looking," Adam told me.

I gulped down a sob, regretting it when the taste of ash coated my tongue and throat heavier than before. Adam moved his injured hand and used his other one to pull me into a hug. He didn't say anything, didn't offer any false assurances. We both knew that it was probably too late for Dante.

A sharp, agonized wail pulled us apart and I turned to see Natalie on the ground, trying to scrabble away from the people around her. River was on a foldout table covered in maps, half a dozen people around her. Two more were crouching with Natalie, clearly trying to treat her as well, but she kept batting away their hands and yelling at them to let her get to River.

"Go," Adam said, gently pushing me in her direction.

I did, moving around to kneel in front of Natalie. Her eyes were wide and bright red, soot streaking her face the same as Adam's. There was something rumpled about her that made it look like she'd been wet. Her arms were red raw, blisters starting to form along them. The skin of her face was red too, but not as much as her arms.

She didn't even seem to see me, all her focus over my shoulder where River lay on the table.

I wanted to take her hand, cup her face, do something to get her attention, but those areas didn't seem safe for me to touch without causing her more pain. Settling for her knee, which was covered by her seemingly untouched jeans, I squeezed it softly.

"Natalie, Natalie look at me," I said. "It's Iris."

There was so much noise. The roar of the fire, the voices of everyone trying to help River. Finally, with a bit more coaxing, Natalie's eyes slid down to me. She didn't speak, though, just stared. Her whole body was trembling.

"Natalie, you need to let them treat you," I urged.

"River."

"River has all the help she needs," I said. I hoped.

"She needs me."

I nodded. "Yes, yes she does. That's why you need to let these other people treat you, okay? So you can be there for her."

This seemed to get through and she nodded, no longer fighting as the firefighters reached for her.

"It'll be okay," I said, patting her knee once before standing up to move out of the way.

Her eyes were focused behind me once more and she didn't respond. My body felt hollowed out, not a single emotion left. Not anger, not fear, not sadness. Two hours ago we'd passed this point laughing and smiling, waving at kids in our dust trail. Now my two best friends were injured, my boyfriend was dead, those kids were homeless or worse, and our other friend had caused all of it.

Even when I turned to look at River, saw burns stretching across her face, no emotions came. Maybe if she hadn't been breathing they would have, but her chest was indeed rising and falling, if only slightly.

It felt like watching a play as everyone raced around, lit in flickering orange. There seemed to be a debate over the single ambulance, which already had one person strapped to the stretcher, another slumped in a foldout seat, and two curled up on the floor. No more room.

Someone slammed the doors on the back of it and it took off. River was still here, though. And Natalie. And Adam. And

Dante, up on the mountainside somewhere. Alone. Gone.

Gone. Gone. Gone.

Idly, I watched as Officer Turner sprinted back to his car and for a moment I thought he'd forgotten about me. But no. He drove closer and swung the SUV around so the rear was facing River's table, only a few feet away. Jumping back out, he popped the trunk open and started chucking stuff from inside onto the ground. With the help of the others around him, River was moved inside, one firefighter crawling in with her.

"Come on," Adam said, gently tugging my elbow. He seemed to have a better grasp of what was going on, so I didn't object as he led me back to the SUV. Opening the backseat, he guided me in next to Toby, then held the door open for someone else to help Natalie in next to me. He closed the door firmly, then went around and slid into the passenger seat I'd occupied before.

Natalie twisted around, face and one hand pressed against the plexiglass divider between her and River. Toby was working so hard not to look at Natalie or River I could feel the tension radiating off of him.

I turned to him, determined to make the pain worse again. To force him to feel what I couldn't anymore. "Dante's dead."

Toby let out a small whimper. "He can't be."

"Well he is. You killed him," I replied.

Adam looked back at us as Officer Turner climbed into the driver's seat. "Iris—"

"Don't. You know he is," I said. "Toby started the fire. It's his fault. He needs to know what he did."

Adam swallowed heavily but didn't say anything else.

"He can't be," Toby whispered. "He's my friend."

I didn't respond.

Officer Turner turned the siren back on and took off. Within moments the heat and roar faded away, leaving only the undulating wail of the siren and the sounds of River barely clinging to life as the firefighter did everything he could to keep her breathing.

Officer Turner: Dispatch, this is Officer Turner. Coming into town with two casualties from the fire, one critical. ETA forty minutes.

Troublesome Dispatch: Copy. Give me an injury run down, I'll pass it on to the hospital.

Officer Turner: Critical patient has severe third-degree burns to the upper half of her face, secondnd and possible third-degree burns on both arms, smoke inhalation, dehydration, and shock. Second patient has second and possible third-degree burns on both arms, smoke inhalation, dehydration, and shock. Both are young women in their late teens.

Troublesome Dispatch: Are they both conscious?

Officer Turner: Only the second patient. I might be able to shave some minutes off my ETA with a clear road into town if we can get someone to stop traffic on the turnoff before I get there.

Troublesome Dispatch: I'll get someone out there. Radio in when you're ten out from the turnoff.

Officer Turner: Copy.

CHAPTER 18: HOSPITAL

Adam

We'd made it. This wasn't over yet, but we'd made it out. There was help now. People to look after River and Natalie, people who knew what they were doing.

The problem, though, was that this gave me time to think. No more shuddering gear shift and stiff wheel demanding my attention. No more baking heat chasing away my thoughts. No more smoke choking my lungs. Just the buzz of the cold road underneath us, and the wail of the siren above.

Yes, I had managed to rescue Natalie and River. Maybe River. But Dante.... And why had no one crossed paths with Shawn? My adrenaline was fading, softening the edges of all my memories, but I didn't think I'd heard him on the radio since he said he was heading straight down into the fire.

It had been my idea to take the trucks. He wouldn't have been there if I hadn't suggested it. Fuck.

Fuck.

Fuck.

I'd never met Shawn's wife, Dante's mother, but a vague picture of her bloomed inside my mind anyways. Was she alone now? Had I gotten her husband killed when her son was also dead? I pictured her standing in her living room, crying and calling her husband and son over and over again, not knowing if they'd ever answer, if she'd ever see them again. Maybe she had the radio on, or the TV, listening to updates about the fire. Maybe she could see the smoke from where they lived, lit up orange by the glow of the fire underneath.

"Don't hurt yourself."

"What?" I gasped, attention being yanked back to the present.

"Don't hurt yourself. Your leg." It was the officer speaking. He didn't look at me, too focused on the road and his speed.

Looking down I realized my unburned hand was clamped so tightly around my knee that my fingers were white. One finger at a time, I released the tension. There'd be bruises there tomorrow. Releasing my hand did not release the tension around my heart, or the circling of my thoughts, however.

Elliot had said taking the trucks was a bad idea. Maybe he was right. Sure, I'd rescued Natalie and maybe River. But not Dante. Not Shawn. People had still been in the Village as well, I'd seen them among the firefighters. What difference had I made, really?

Maybe if I'd stayed in the Village I could have done more good there. Saved someone's house. Convinced more people to leave. Something. What if there'd been people there who couldn't evacuate there either? Someone in a wheelchair, or with a car that wouldn't start? Had I left people there to die when I could have saved them?

Or maybe I could have held the line until the real firefighters showed up. I didn't know a damn thing about firefighting aside from "throw water at it," and I'd only had the one tanker, but the thought still dragged at me. How could I ever know that my one tanker of water might not have been just enough to dampen the ground ahead of the fire to the point the plants could have held on a little longer?

"Officer Turner, I'm ten minutes out from the turnoff."

"Copy, closing the road down now."

No one else spoke, aside from an occasional murmur from the firefighter trying to save River. Toby was silent and every time I glanced back, he was just staring dazedly at his knees. Natalie remained twisted around to watch River. Iris sat between them, eyes tired and hollow.

The cop slowed to take the turn towards town, fishtailing a bit anyway. Though he'd radioed for another cop to block traffic to give us a clear shot down the road, that wasn't who was doing it. It was just a county road maintenance truck, battered and dinged with a man in an orange vest standing next to it, illuminated by the headlights of a line of cars waiting behind him. On a paved surface now, we sped up down the long straightaway.

"Officer Turner, two minutes out from the hospital."

"Copy, a team is waiting for you, they've opened the old ambulance doors."

The old ambulance doors?

Oh.

The hospital was under renovation.

Oh.

Oh no.

The place was small enough on its own, only a handful of beds and a barebones emergency department. The biggest part of the whole place was the nursing home and elderly care wing. How much was still open? Still usable? What had been closed down for construction?

Smoother than I'd thought possible at our speed, the SUV came to a stop directly in front of the ambulance bay doors. Cones had been chucked haphazardly into the bushes, plywood laid down where the asphalt had been torn up. Three people were waiting with a stretcher, bringing it around to the back and loading River onto it. With the old ramp torn out, the only way to get River inside was for everyone to manually lift her whole stretcher up a foot, the cop and firefighter leaping out to help.

Natalie was sobbing, desperately slamming against her door, unable to open it from the inside. I didn't have that problem in the front though, so I got out, struggling to get my legs under me. Maybe I was in shock too. Maybe I was just exhausted. I couldn't tell.

I went around and pulled the latch, catching Natalie as she tumbled out, trying to be careful of any injuries she might have. She fought to get away from me, clawing at my arms and trying to wiggle past. I knew I had to be hurting her, that she had to be hurting herself, but I didn't think it was a good idea to let her just run off into the hospital on her own. I managed to keep her in place until Iris was out as well, making sure Iris had an arm around Natalie's waist before letting Natalie go.

One hand still on the door, I looked inside at Toby. Natalie said he'd started this. So had Iris. Now it made sense why he'd stayed in the truck when I ran into him and Iris earlier, why he hadn't been as insistent as her on staying. He didn't say a word, and he didn't look surprised when I shut the door.

The cop passed me as I went inside, his face grim. We glanced at one another and then I left him to deal with Toby as I went inside. The hospital was in chaos. There were dozens of people, some with obvious injuries and many that just looked panicked. In one corner a baby was wailing in their carrier, the woman rocking the carrier crying just as hard. A man lay on the floor, one of his legs elevated on a chair, bare foot swollen and purple. Someone else was trembling from head to toe and repeatedly asking for her daughter. The reception desk was missing half its desktop, and the walls were still taped off around a fresh coat of pale blue paint. None of the chairs matched or had any sort of order. It was like they'd all just been dragged in haphazardly.

Nurses darted from person to person, asking questions and scribbling notes. Several elderly people from the attached nursing home seemed to have wandered in as well and appeared to be going around comforting people. I recognized a few of them from taking my sisters trick-or-treating through their rooms. Lillian, a whip-smart lady in her 80s, went over to the crying baby and mother, scooping the baby out of the carrier. She sat next to the mother, rocking the baby in one arm and patting the mother's back with the other. Frank, a former farmer in his 90s, puttered about in his wheelchair, handing out sweets from a tin on his lap. Even the nursing home cat had decided this was where she needed to be, weaving her way between everyone's legs and loving on them.

I had no idea where to go, instead hovering in the doorway. Probably I should do something about my hand. Find a place to run it under cool water. Knowing didn't seem to translate into doing, though, so I continued to stand there. Only when the cop came through from behind, one hand on Toby's upper arm, did

I step aside. A few people glanced at Toby, but no one seemed to care that a handcuffed teen was in their midst. Would they react the same if they knew what he'd done?

The officer took Toby to a nurse, asking her for a clear health sign-off so Toby could be taken in and booked. Not caring if Toby was healthy or not, I went back to looking around. Maybe I should find Iris. She shouldn't be alone, and Natalie wasn't in any state to comfort her.

This thought finally got me moving, but I was unsure where to go. I wandered towards one of the sets of double doors I could see that led deeper into the hospital. Both doors had been propped open, and in the hallway beyond nurses darted from room to room, calling out codes and medications and stats. I hesitated, trying to figure out if I was allowed to enter, or where to even go if I did.

"Adam."

I turned and saw Iris and Natalie in the first room, Iris looking at me while Natalie just stared vacantly ahead, lips forming words I couldn't hear from this distance. No one tried to stop me as I strode into the room. Natalie was sitting on a bed, Iris next to her, trying to console her. Despite having her in my truck for the run out of the fire, and riding with her back to town, this was the first time I got a good look at Natalie. Her hair was singed, hanging in tangled chunks around her face which had what seemed like a horrible sunburn. Along her arms the burns were even worse, blisters beginning to fill up with fluid. A monitor next to the bed beeped rapidly, reflecting Natalie's jackrabbit heart rate. Iris was trying to soothe her as a nurse treated Natalie's arms.

"Can I...help?" I asked.

Iris looked at me, eyes still almost expressionless despite the state of her friend. Whatever Dante had meant to her, she wasn't handling him being gone well. "She needs oxygen, and fluids, but they're out of masks and nearly out of IV bags too."

"More ambulances are on the way to transfer the worst cases, and bring us more supplies," the nurse said. I realized she wasn't in scrubs, but in fuzzy PJ pants and a ratty t-shirt. All that singled her out as a nurse was the stethoscope around her neck and the gloves she had on.

Natalie was babbling, saying River's name over and over again, mixed in with fractured sentences about running and the pond and exploding trees. With Iris and the nurse refocused on her, I shrunk back out of the room until I hit the far wall of the hallway. A renewed sense of uselessness washed over me in waves. I hadn't saved Dante. I might not have saved River. I'd likely gotten Shawn killed. I hadn't gotten everyone out of the Village. I hadn't even found Natalie quick enough to get her the help she needed before the supplies ran out.

Sometime later an empty stretcher rolled by several paramedics directing it, then another that was rolled into Natalie's room. The second one also came with a team of paramedics who immediately started helping the nurse. Iris slipped out to stand with me, both of us watching Natalie get oxygen, a new IV bag, and sedation. They strapped her to the stretcher and brought her out, taking her away down the hall. River followed a moment later, most of her face and arms covered in thick bandages.

"Now what?" Iris asked into the empty hallway.

"Are either of you hurt?" the nurse asked, looking at us both while focusing more on me. I didn't know what I looked like but I imagined it wasn't good. Iris had some soot down the left side of her face, and a few smears of it elsewhere, but aside from that she seemed okay.

Wordlessly I held out my burned hand. Stripping off her old gloves in favor of a new pair, the nurse gently examined my palm and fingers.

"Not too bad, mostly first degree, little bit of second. Come back in the room, I'll get you some burn cream and bandages."

I followed her and Iris came with. Now that Natalie and River were gone, she seemed like a balloon cut loose. Just floating about as things bumped into her.

The burn cream stung for a moment as it reminded the nerves of their battered state, but soon the sensation faded, replaced by a cool relief. Several minutes later my hand was a mitten of bandages.

"Okay," the nurse said, looking at both of us again. Iris was hovering at the end of the bed. "We need this room, so I'm going to send you two back to the waiting room, but you are not discharged yet, understood?"

We both nodded.

"And I'm giving you both a job, okay? You need to watch one another, make sure the other is doing alright."

We both nodded.

Together we went to the waiting room. There weren't chairs available, so we found a corner and sat on the floor. The panic seemed to have subsided somewhat, thanks, it seemed, to the efforts of those from the nursing home. A softly smiling old woman I thought might be named Margret came by with a cart, handing us some water bottles and granola bars. Our spot afforded us a perfect view of the ambulance bay doors, the people being brought out and the supplies being brought in.

"I don't know what watching one another is supposed to mean," Iris said.

"I think she just wants us to have something else to focus on. A task to do."

Iris slid her eyes over to me without really turning her head. "Like sending me to the Village?"

I managed a small smile. "Yeah. Like that."

Iris nodded. "Adam?"

"Hmm?"

"Why were you out there?"

I glanced at her. She wasn't looking at me anymore, eyes focused on the activity around us.

"We saw it start, up at the mine," I said. "We had the water trucks for road maintenance, and I thought...I thought that we'd get there so much quicker than the fire department. That we could put it out before it got bad." I almost mentioned Dante's dad, stopping myself before I did. That would involve mentioning Dante, and I wasn't sure Iris could handle that right now. "By the time I got down from the mine and headed up, it was already beyond anything our little water trucks could do.

But I knew there were people missing up there, so I kept going."

"Oh." Iris went silent for several minutes. "Thank you."

"I'm not sure how much of a difference it actually made," I admitted, needing to say it out loud.

"At least you tried," Iris offered. "I was just as ready to go back in there as you were, and I was much less prepared. At the very, very least you kept Toby and me from getting killed. And you did get River and Natalie out, even if they were hurt."

"I suppose." Maybe I'd believe her later, with some distance from the event. But right now her words felt hollow.

"I'm...I'm sorry about Dante," I said hesitantly, a little while later.

She took a shaky breath. "He stayed to try and save River and Natalie, same as you."

"Were you two together?" I asked carefully. Dante and I hadn't talked since I dropped out of school, so I wasn't sure. But I knew he'd had a crush on her.

She sniffed and nodded, tears welling in her eyes.

Unsure what else to say, I put an arm around her shoulders, giving her a side hug. She sniffed again and leaned into me, resting her head on my shoulder. The ambulance doors continued to open and close, the exchange of injured people and supplies seemingly unending. Without warning, the doors burst open quicker than before, smacking into the walls and making several people jump. This time it wasn't supplies being rushed in. It was someone on a stretcher, a firefighter kneeling over them and doing chest compressions.

Iris sat up, a confused look on her face before her eyes went wide and she leaped up, darting for the stretcher as it was whisked by. My mind caught up a second later, recognizing Dante's battered form. Racing after Iris, I snagged her around the waist, catching her right outside the room they'd taken Dante to. She struggled against me, calling out Dante's name over and over, tears racing down her cheeks.

"Don't get in the way," I said, holding her tightly against me. "Let them work, let them work."

She stopped struggling, her body trembling violently. I kept my arms around her just as much for comfort as for restraint.

Half a dozen people were working on Dante, alternating CPR and shocking him with a defibrillator until his heart did something they agreed with. More motion, more shouting, more dashing. A tube was slid down his throat. Iris trembled harder. Or maybe it was me.

"He made it this far," I whispered into her hair. "He made it this far."

CHAPTER 19: REUNION

Adam's arms around me were the only thing keeping me together. The idea of Dante being dead had been insurmountable. The thought of waiting days or weeks for his body to be found excruciating. The reality of never seeing his face again terrifying. I'd expected it, though. Turned it over and over in my mind ever since I realized he wasn't in Adam's truck. But seeing Dante wheeled in on a stretcher, a sooty firefighter kneeled over him doing CPR so hard it looked like his chest was being caved in? That wasn't something I could comprehend.

Knowing what real, non-Hollywood CPR entailed and actually seeing it were two very different things. There was no way that could be helpful, right? There was no way it could fix anything. A real person's chest couldn't be caved in like that over and over.

I wanted this to be over. I wanted things to stop happening, to stop piling up and up and up. It wasn't that I wanted Dante to be dead, of course I didn't. But it was easier when he had been, when I hadn't had to see it happening. He was out of view now, though, curtains drawn around his bed as the doctors and nurses worked, starting the process of wondering and fearing all over again.

Adam gently tugged me back to our corner, guiding me to the floor before kneeling in front of me.

"He's strong," Adam said. "In shape, I mean. From football. And young. That counts for a lot."

"He wants to be a firefighter," I said, still watching over Adam's shoulder. "That's...that's the only reason he joined the football team. So he could stay in shape." Was that even a possibility anymore? Or had this entire ordeal stolen away his dreams?

"Good. Gives him something to aim for while he's getting better," Adam said.

"What's with you and your distracting goals?" I asked, aware that distracting myself was exactly what I was doing right now.

He gave a sad smile and a little shrug. "It was part of therapy after my parents died."

"Oh. I knew you lived with your aunt and uncle, but...."

"They died in a car crash three years ago. Went over the edge in a blizzard," Adam said.

"I'm sorry."

"Me too."

"How'd you distract yourself?" I asked. As long as we were talking there wasn't room to think about Dante. Much.

"Spoiling my little sisters, mostly. Isabella and Cory. I wrote a lot too." He had one hand on my knee, softly running his thumb back and forth. It occurred to me that this was what I'd done for Natalie earlier.

"What do you write?"

"Poetry. Don't know if it's any good, though. I've never shared it with anyone."

"Iris!" A voice called out from the other side of the room.

Straightening up I looked around, spotting my mom weaving her way over. Adam moved aside as I leapt up and hurled myself into her arms. She held me back just as tightly, petting my hair and crying.

"Oh, honey, how long have you been here? We've been trying to call you!" she said.

"I dunno," I said, choking on the words. "I don't even know where my phone is right now." Maybe still in River's truck?

She pulled back, arms still around me, looking at me with a worried frown. It was only then that I realized more people had come in with her. Natalie's parents, River's parents, and Dante's mother were all standing there, looking equally worried, all glancing around for their own children.

I looked at Adam with wide eyes, no idea what to do. Had

no one from the hospital called them? No one from the police station? Told them their kids were hurt? The idea of being the one to do that seemed impossible. Adam looked just as lost.

"Iris, honey, what happened?" my mom asked, voice tentative, like she didn't want to spook me. "Dante's mom called us all, a couple hours ago, said her husband called from the mine to say there was a fire where you five went camping. And I got that text from you saying you were okay, but you never texted or called after that. Then, just a bit ago, Toby's parents got a call that he was at the police station?" Her hands were cupped around my face now, worry still evident in every bit of her expression.

Adam had gone stiff next to us, his eyes focused on the floor.

"I—we—Toby started the fire," I stuttered out. "It blew up so fast. And—And—we got separated. Natalie and River weren't with us when it started, and Dante went to find them—and— and—" I couldn't get the rest out, my breath hitching in my chest.

"I was at the mine with Shawn," Adam spoke up. He was looking at Dante's mom now, shoulders square and sorrow in his eyes. "We all saw the fire start from the parking lot and called it in. When Shawn realized that Dante and his friends were up there he and I stole two of the mine water tender trucks to try and go find them. Neither of us had any idea how bad the fire was going to get, how quickly it would blow up, but we both made the decision to keep going." Adam took a shaky breath. "I found River and Natalie eventually, they'd taken shelter in a pond, but they were both hurt. I didn't find Dante, but a crew of firefighters did, and...I don't know what happened to Shawn. He stopped responding on the radio before I even found River and Natalie, and we never crossed paths where we should have based on the roads we each took."

Silence followed his statement. I could see Adam cracking under the pressure of the quiet, but he never broke eye contact with Dante's mom.

"I'm sorry," Adam whispered.

"Where's my son?" Dante's mom asked, voice shaking.

River's dad put an arm around her shoulders.

"They brought him in and took him back to a room a few minutes ago," Adam answered. "They were doing CPR, that's all I know."

Dante's mom let out a little wail, collapsing against River's dad.

Adam took another deep breath and continued. "River had burns on her arms and bad ones on her face as well. Natalie also had burns, but they were mostly on her arms. They were both taken away by ambulance a little while ago, but I don't know where they were taken."

Nearly everyone was making some sort of pained noise now and I couldn't take it, tucking myself back against my mom, hands over my ears. She held me tight, stroking my hair over and over.

A nurse seemed to finally realize that the parents of injured children were in their midst and our group was shepherded to a different, smaller, waiting room. The nurses apologized profusely for not calling, saying things had been too chaotic and treating everyone took precedence. River's dad seemed to be stepping in to take control of the situation. He'd found out where River and Natalie were taken, helped arrange for someone to watch Natalie's little brother so both her parents could go to the city to be with her. He'd gotten hold of Dante's aunt as well, telling her what was happening and that her sister needed her. She lived three hours away, though, so it would be a while before she arrived.

My dad appeared right as River and Natalie's parents left, all of them requesting that my mom keep them up to date on what was happening here. Dad scooped me up, holding me as tight as my mom had and apologizing for taking so long to make it over the pass from where he'd been called to tow a car. I didn't have any energy left to hold him back, hardly able to even stay awake now. He and my mother conversed in soft tones, checking in with Dante's mom now and then.

Adam remained with us, a bit off to the side. He'd used my

mom's phone to call his aunt and uncle, informing them he was fine, just staying at the hospital to support some friends. He didn't mention his hand, nor that he'd driven through the fire.

How long had we been here? I didn't know anymore. Whatever I was feeling now was something beyond tired. A strange, floating, flickering awareness. Only when a nurse came in and sat down did I pull myself back to full attention.

"Dante is stable," he said.

A whimper echoed out into the room, but I couldn't tell if it was from me or Dante's mom. Maybe both.

The nurse continued, "He has burns to his arms, hands, and back, and some damage to his lungs, though we aren't sure of the extent of the lung damage yet. He was also dangerously dehydrated, suffering from heatstroke, and suffering from smoke inhalation. On the way to the hospital he stopped breathing, and CPR was performed, resulting in several broken ribs."

Dante's mother had her hands clasped to her mouth, her eyes clenched shut. Tears still made their way out, though, rolling down her cheeks.

"Is he being taken to the city too?" I asked.

The nurse nodded. "Yes, now that he's stable. Another ambulance is on the way to pick him up. It should be here soon."

"Can I see him?" I pleaded.

The nurse looked to Dante's mother who managed a little nod.

"Okay," the nurse said, standing up. "It has to be brief, though, and we only have room for a couple people."

My dad squeezed my hand. "We'll be right here, sweetheart."

I squeezed back, then followed the nurse and Dante's mother. He led us down several hallways, stopping at a room with a single bed. Dante was on it, but it didn't quite look like him. His arms were covered in bandages from fingertips to shoulders, a tube was in his throat, and his skin looked gray. Another nurse was watching over him, monitoring his vitals and fidgeting with all the tubes and cords trailing from him.

Dante's mom stumbled forward, collapsing into a chair

next to the bed, body convulsing with emotions she could not contain. I couldn't make it beyond the doorway. Where was my boyfriend? The strong, funny, sweet guy whose hugs always made me feel safe? We were supposed to share a tent tonight. Sleep under the stars. This couldn't be him. He looked so small.

A hand settled gently between my shoulder blades. I looked over to see the nurse who had brought us in smiling at me sympathetically.

"Come on," he said, guiding me towards the opposite side of the bed from Dante's mom. Once there, the nurse took my hand and rested it on the blankets over Dante's leg, then stepped back to give me a little space.

"Hi," I managed, my voice cracking on the word. "Hi, love." What was I supposed to say? "River and Natalie are safe." Yeah, he'd want to know that. "Adam rescued them, the guy you used to tutor sometimes. Toby's...safe, too. They arrested him. We all made it out, okay? We made it out, and you did too."

Getting only silence in return was excruciating. I wanted to see him open his eyes, tease me about being so worried. It wasn't going to happen, though. Not for a while, anyway.

With nothing else to say, I kissed my fingers and then gently tapped them against his shoulder, the only place that seemed somewhat safe to touch other than where the nurse had placed my hand on his leg. "I love you."

911 Dispatch: Trouble—

Caller: Help me, please, please! My house is burning!

911 Dispatch: Sir we're doing the best we can.

Caller: That's what everyone's been saying and nobody is here!

911 Dispatch: Sir, you need to run. Just run.

Caller: We're suffocating!

Caller: We're gonna die in here. My son is with me, please! He's only 12! Please! We got turned around in the smoke.

Captain Henderson: We're pulling out. Too many trees in there. It's not safe. Clear the last house and get out.

Engine 41: Copy that. Who's last out?

Engine 62: We are; engine 62.

Captain Henderson: Watch yourselves.

Caller: Our car is stuck! Our car is stuck! Please! We just got married, my wife can't breathe. Please. Please. Please.

Engine 62: Reverse and move! Reverse and move! The wind is back! Reverse and move!

Captain Henderson: Everyone call in! Henderson crew truck, clear out.

Engine 41: 41, clear out.

Engine 42: 42, clear out.

Engine 6: 6, clear out.

Engine 8: 8, clear out.

Officer Monir: Officer Monir, clear out.

Engine 12: 12, clear out.

Officer Black: Officer Black, clear out.

Captain Henderson: 62, do you copy? Are you cleared out?

Captain Henderson: 62, do you copy? Are you cleared out? Someone relay.

Engine 41: 62 are you clear out?

Officer Black: 62 are you clear out?

Captain Henderson: Who saw them last?

Engine 8: They were behind 8 on the north side of the Village, but it was burning over bad. They may have stopped and deployed heat shields.

Captain Henderson: 62, do you acknowledge?

Captain Henderson: 62, do you acknowledge?

Captain Henderson: 62, please acknowledge. Please.

◎ Lorelei Deady
15minutes ago | Public

ATTENTION EVERYONE! THREAD FOR ASSISTING EVACUEES!

Please use this as a space to collect immediate resource offers for evacuees! If you have open beds in your homes, campers people can borrow, storage people can use, space to house animals, anything, post about it below. Once the resource is taken, please edit your initial post to say so. #LostHenFire #TroublesomeStrong

☹ 👍 ♡ ✾ 608

◎ Tom Espinoza
Got three stalls at my barn. DM me.

👍 ♡ 24

◎ Jenny Sparrow
We have an open mother-in-law suite above our garage. Two bedrooms, one bath, full kitchen. Available to whoever needs it for as long as they need it. Call 970-555-8935

Edit: Claimed. We have some additional room in our garage for storage.

👍 ♡ 68

◎ Veronica Evans
The church on Main and Leaf St. is open and serving food. If anyone has camp cots or other portable bedding they'd be willing to loan us please call 970-555-6892 or come drop it off.

☹ 👍 ♡ 102

⬡ **George Cantrell**

We've got a fifth wheel in the backyard. Hooked up to power and water. Call 970-555-5236.

👍 ♡ 28

⬡ **Sadie's Hill Veterinary Care**

We're providing free boarding for pets. If anyone has food they can donate, it would be appreciated! 10 spots for dogs, 20 for cats, 5-10 for livestock animals depending on the animal.

Edit: 3 dog spots left, 12 for cats, 2 for livestock.

👍 ♡ ✹ 72

ZERO TO 80,000 ACRES IN ONE NIGHT; 14 DEAD

A wildfire sparked by a carelessly lit campfire destroyed 80,000 acres of Troublesome County overnight and continues to burn with 0% containment. There are currently fourteen known fatalities, including six firefighters whose engine stalled as the fire burned over them, preventing escape. The other eight include five people from the Miner's Village neighborhood, one man from the Molly Mine, and a young couple who had been staying in a rented cabin in the area for their honeymoon. No names will be released at this time, pending notification of their families. Specific causes of death are also being withheld at this time.

While we will not be naming him at this time, we would like to acknowledge that the man from the Molly Mine helped rescue a family of campers when their car went off the road as they attempted to escape the fire. The family is confirmed to have made it out alive. His heroism will be remembered, and honored, at a later date.

Firefighters from across the state continue to fight the fire, with resources coming in from across the country as well. There is, unfortunately, still no rain in the upcoming forecasts. Due to the terrain and the weather, options for fighting the fire are limited.

One seventeen-year-old juvenile has been arrested on charges of arson for starting the fire. It is believed further charges will be forthcoming. His name has not been released due to his age, but it is likely that he will be tried as an adult.

For those wishing to make a donation to those displaced by the fire, there are donation boxes set out at all county government offices and both county libraries. There is a high need for diapers, feminine products, food for pets, and stuffed animals or other small toys and comfort items for children.

For those wishing to make a donation to first responders, they are not currently accepting donations. The fire crews are well supplied. However, the fire camp is looking for volunteers to help with meal prep. Please contact 970-555-6801 for more information.

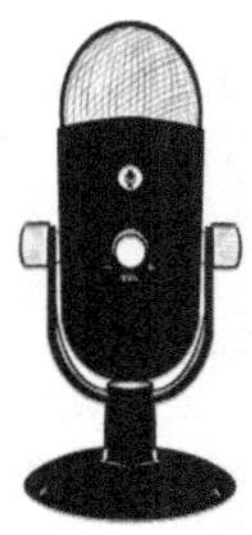

Radio Host: Captain Henderson, I know the fire has now been handed off to several wildland teams, but can you give any insight into the future of this fire?

Captain Henderson: Honestly? No. I've been at this for 25 years, my father for 50 before he retired, and my grandfather for 48. None of us have ever, had ever, seen anything like this fire. It has done things we didn't think fire could do. It is being fought with every possible resource and technique, but we just don't know.

Radio Host: That's a scary thing to hear.

Captain Henderson: It's supposed to be. This fire started because someone was careless and didn't think the fire ban applied to them. Hopefully, this fire will show exactly why it *does* apply to everyone, no matter how careful they think they are being.

Radio Host: Is there an explanation for why this one was so bad? It can't just be climate change, can it? None of the other fires around the state right now have done this.

Captain Henderson: It was probably a lot of factors that all came together in the worst possible way. The fire started just as a windstorm came in. The area was hit hard by the beetles fifteen years ago, and had wind funneling directly into where the fire started, allowing it to get a large, quick foothold. Much of the terrain is rugged and hard to work in. Climate change built the pyre, a careless person lit the match, and everything else did the rest.

Radio Host: And, about the rumors circulating that one or more of your crews took unnecessary risks to rescue someone due to personal connections, do you have any comment?

Captain Henderson: Look, this is a small town. A small county. Everyone has a personal connection with everyone. If we avoided dangerous situations just because we might know the people involved, we wouldn't be able to go out on a single call. While the risks taken may look excessive in hindsight, I have full faith in the judgement of my crews in the moment, personal connections or not.

Radio Host: Fair enough. If you could have people take something away from all of this, aside from respecting the fire bans, what would it be?

Captain Henderson: I think…it would be that there will always be help. We have seen and continue to see some extraordinary acts of heroism both on the fire lines, and back home, to get people out and then make sure they had a place to go, and the support they needed once they got there. This isn't some Hollywood film where everyone turned on one another, this is the real world. There will always be people ready to give everything to help those around them.

To: Adam.J.Delgado@CMail.com
From: DKristofferson@TCHS.com
Subject: My dad

Hey Adam. Iris sent me your e-mail. I would've
called, but talking too much still hurts. They
officially identified my dad's body today, and
I was just…I was kind of hoping you could tell
me what happened? I mean. I know what happened,
I know you two took the trucks and came to find
us. I know my dad went one way and you went the
other. I know his truck stalled and then blew up.
People have told me all of that. But…can you tell
me…I don't know, what he said? Please?

———

To: DKristofferson@TCHS.com
From: Adam.J.Delgado@CMail.com
Re: My dad

Of course I can. I'm so sorry he didn't make it
out.

Your dad wanted to save your life. He was
desperate to figure out where you were, figure
out a way to protect you. I was the one who took
the keys to the tenders and gave him a set. He
went first down the road, and after that I only
heard from him on the radios a few times. As much
as he wanted to get to you, he still stopped to
help a family whose car got stuck. I don't know

who they were, but based on what the paper said
they made it out alive.

I don't know if it was the last thing he said,
but the last time I heard him over the radios he
was at the top of the ridge between the mine and
Lost Hen. He told us the fire was bad, but he
was going in anyway because you were out there.
Elliot, our boss, tried to talk him out of it but
your dad never responded.

I've spent the last couple weeks wondering if I
did the right thing, stealing those keys. Giving
him a set. I'm not saying that because I want
sympathy from you, far from it. I just…I want you
to know it isn't something I'm taking lightly. He
went out there for you, but he was in that truck
because of me.

I'm so sorry.

———

To: Adam.J.Delgado@CMail.com
From: DKristofferson@TCHS.com
Re: Re: My dad

Thank you.

And…honestly…he probably would've just gotten in
his own car and taken that to find us. He was
that kind of guy.

It's funny, well, not funny, but for awhile I
was trapped on a rock ledge. It looked out over
the whole gully. I was pretty delirious at that
point, but I saw his headlights, coming down the
other side. I didn't know it was him, of course,
but I imagined that it was. Imagined him rescuing
me off the side of the mountain and taking me
home. Knowing it was actually him is kind of
comforting, even though I also saw the truck blow
up.

It's all a lot. I don't really know how I feel
about any of it, or if I ever will. But I
don't blame you, Adam, and you shouldn't blame
yourself. My dad wouldn't want you to either. He
wasn't that kind of guy.

Dad was cremated, but Mom is waiting to have the
memorial until after I'm out of the hospital,
so we don't have a solid date yet, but will you
come? It'll probably just be at the church.

———

To: DKristofferson@TCHS.com
From: Adam.J.Delgado@CMail.com
Re: Re: Re: My dad

"I don't really know how I feel about any of
it, or if I ever will." Same. None of this quite
feels real. I know it happened, I remember all
of it, even if it has gone a little fuzzy, but…
it sort of feels like something I watched on TV.
Or maybe something I watched on TV and then had a
dream about.

And yeah. I'll come, as long as your mom is okay
with it. How is she?

———

To: Adam.J.Delgado@CMail.com
From: DKristofferson@TCHS.com
Re: Re: Re: Re: My dad

She's…struggling. My aunt is helping out
with everything, though, and it makes a big
difference. And yes, she'll be okay with it. She
hasn't talked much about what happened, at least
to me, but she has said that she understands what
he did.

Also, I should've said it before, but thank you
for finding River and Natalie and getting them

out. And for being there for Iris as much as you
were. It still amazes me that all four of us, and
Toby, made it out alive.

But anyway, the nurse is scolding me for being on
my tablet, so I've gotta go. I'll let you know
about my dad's funeral.

———

To: DKristofferson@TCHS.com
From: Adam.J.Delgado@CMail.com
Re: Re: Re: Re: Re: My dad

Sounds good. Hope your recovery keeps going well.

CHAPTER 20: REMEMBRANCE

Five Weeks Later

A soft breeze fluttered the yellow ribbons adorning each tree and post along Mainstreet. Every business had signs in their windows thanking the local firefighters. Clapboards sat along the sidewalk, directing people to the donation centers set up for those who had been displaced by the fire. Only a haze of smoke remained visible off to the south, the dying gasps of the blaze that, all told, had consumed roughly 180,000 acres so far. Containment was at 65%, but until there was a long-lasting solid blanket of snow no one would quite feel safe. There'd been a little rain, at least, which was something.

The one cafe in town was bursting at the seams, people going inside to order at the counter before taking their food to sit outside on the town square lawn. All but one table at the cafe was taken, even the ones outside in the late September sun. That table, though, had a little placard on it stating it was reserved, and it was the only one with an umbrella, though it was closed. Five chairs had been crammed in around the table despite it only really having room for three. Whoever sat there would have to be okay with knocking elbows.

Adam was the first to show up, his little sisters trailing along with him, one holding his hand and the other with her fingers twisted in one of his belt loops, afraid to hold his mostly healed other hand. He gave them each a kiss on the top of their heads, handed them a twenty to get lunch, and told them to stay in the square. They dashed inside, giggling, as Adam went and cranked open the umbrella. One spot, the one that put his back to the street, was still in the sun and he took that one, settling in to wait.

Iris arrived next, strolling down the street, looking tired but relatively happy. She leaned down to hug Adam before taking the other seat that caught a few rays of sun. Immediately after the fire they hadn't talked, too caught up in what was happening, but over the last few weeks they'd been texting a lot. It helped, having someone else going through the same process of sorting out their feelings about what had happened.

A waitress came out and Iris ordered for everyone else, excluding Adam. She didn't order much, doubting anyone would have much of an appetite. A large plate of fries and a few sodas would probably be enough. Adam agreed, only getting himself a soda as well.

When Dante walked into her view Iris immediately lit up. Dante, arms covered to protect his still healing burns, leaned down and gave her a long kiss before taking a seat in the shade, scooting his chair closer to Iris's. If you didn't know that his sleeves were actually a compression garment to help reduce scarring, you'd never know he was recovering from anything, let alone something so horrific. Mostly he just looked tired. Adam had warred with himself about going to Shawn's funeral earlier in the week, only coming along when Dante insisted. They'd been e-mailing a lot and Dante had made it clear that he didn't blame Adam in any way. Adam still blamed himself, though. Just a bit.

Finally, a battered blue hatchback pulled up to the curb a few feet away from the table. The three of them at the table turned to watch as Natalie got out of the back. Her hair had been cut to her shoulders, curling attractively around her face. Compression sleeves ran the lengths of her arms as well and her face still looked somewhat raw.

Reaching back into the car, she helped River step out. Of the five of them, River was the one who most obviously looked like she'd been through a tragedy. In addition to compression garments on her arms, she had one on her face to help reduce the scarring on her forehead and cheeks, as well as a pair of dark sunglasses that concealed and protected her eyes where the compression garment couldn't reach. She'd cut her hair as well, but the style was hard to distinguish due to how all her hair was threaded through the back of the garment over her face. One hand firmly in Natalie's, she snapped open a long white cane in the other.

Probably, Natalie, River, and Dante shouldn't have been there and instead inside somewhere where the sun couldn't hit their healing skin. River had only been discharged from the burn center in the city the evening before. But none of them were willing to miss today, nor were they willing to watch from inside one of the shops along the street.

"Be safe, honey," River's mom said, leaning out from the passenger window.

"Have Natalie text us if you need anything," her dad added.

River smiled. "Of course."

"We've got her," Natalie said, gesturing back to their friends.

River's parents looked nervous but still pulled away, going to park on a side street.

Natalie gently guided River into the outdoor seating area and the chair that Adam pulled out, making sure River was settled before taking the last spot for herself.

Silence hung over them all until River blew a raspberry. "Come on, I'm blind now and even I can see the awkward at this table."

As icebreakers went it wasn't the best, but it worked, snapping the tension and turning it into relieved laughter.

"Missed you, River," Dante said.

River grinned. "Of course you did. How have y'all been? Don't make me call out your names one by one to get you to talk."

Natalie huffed, rolling her eyes lovingly.

"Well," Iris started, "my parents agreed to let me use my college fund for gender-affirmation surgery instead."

"The words sound good, but your tone implies otherwise," River returned.

Iris sighed, fiddling with a fry from the recently arrived plate rather than eating it. "It's...I wanted it so much, but getting it this way just feels...tainted, I guess? I don't know. I'm still trying to sort it out."

Dante put an arm around her shoulders, pulling her in to kiss the top of her head. She snuggled closer, eyes closed in contentment. He kept his arm around her as he caught the others up on his own injuries and recovery.

"My doctor says I might still have a shot at qualifying as a smokejumper, if I'm strict about my PT for my lungs. If not I'll figure out some other way to join up. Operations management or dispatch something," he explained.

Natalie shook her head, swallowing heavily. "I can't believe you even want to try. I can't even light a candle without having a panic attack."

Dante sighed. "Don't get me wrong, what I can remember of everything is terrifying but that's why I want to do it. I want to use what happened to me to help make sure it doesn't happen to other people."

"Me too," Adam said. "Finding a way to use this to help other people, I mean."

If you'd asked Adam before if he wanted to be a firefighter he would've said no. He still wasn't sure that was the actual answer to the clawing need for knowledge he'd felt ever since the day of the fire, but it was one option he'd put on the table. He just wanted to understand. What could he have done differently? Was there a line he could have held somewhere? Had he even used the hose right when cutting a path for River and Natalie, or had he just gotten lucky? Could he have saved more lives in the Village by using different wording when he told them to get out? Probably at least some of these answers had the potential to make him feel worse, to show that he had made the wrong decisions at points. But he still needed to know. If he knew, maybe next time he'd be able to save more people, make more of a difference.

Dante raised his glass and clinked it to Adam's.

"So you're going to join some firefighting crew too?" Iris asked Adam.

He shrugged. "Haven't quite decided yet. I honestly don't know that much about actual firefighting, what sort of jobs there are beyond 'shoot water at hot things.' Might have to pick Dante's brain later."

"Hit me up anytime," Dante offered.

Adam nodded.

"I heard the mine tried to charge you with stealing the truck," River said, earning a lot of indignant spluttering from the rest of the table.

"Oh, they did," Adam said. He was still sort of surprised he hadn't been arrested for it. Part of him suspected the cops had just been too busy with the fire to notice. That hadn't stopped the mine owners, however. They'd been more than happy to press charges for theft and threaten to sue for damages. "Someone posted about it online, though, and got the whole world up in arms about it. Mine ended up dropping all the charges and giving me a year's pay as severance to make all the bad press go away."

"Dicks," Iris declared.

"Can't believe that place survived," Natalie said. "They only lost, what, one administrative building?"

"Yep," Adam said.

"It makes sense," Dante interjected. "All their buildings are concrete, plus they had a huge parking lot between the fire and the main structures. When the fire hit the lot there was nothing for it to burn, so it just ran around."

"Tell that to my car," Adam complained. "I was parked on the edge of the lot. The thing was a total loss. Nothing but a charred shell left."

"Ouch, sorry," Iris said.

"Our valiant vehicles will be forever remembered," River declared, holding up her glass to everyone. "To Adam's car, my truck's transmission, and that indestructible little water tender."

Everyone clinked and drank, Iris apologizing about the transmission.

"Not like I can drive it now anyway," River said nonchalantly. Everyone else seemed a bit uncomfortable with the mild joke, but the moment passed without comment.

Iris was fiddling with another fry. "I wish I'd known about the extinguisher you had in the toolbox."

"It is what it is," River said. "Maybe it would've made a difference, maybe it wouldn't have."

"Still...you're the one who was...was most affected by this," Iris said nervously.

River sighed, leaning back in her chair. "Yeah, I suppose. It's weird. I think my parents are taking it harder than me. Like this cane,"—she jiggled the long white stick—"I don't have any damn clue how to use it yet, but they freak if I don't lug it around. They've dived into the deep end of recovery options. There's already been talks about everything from a transplant to a guide dog. It's a little tiring, honestly. I know they mean well, but...." She trailed off.

"Would a transplant be an option?" Adam asked.

"Maybe," Natalie said. "The way her doctors put it, the data transfer from her eyes still works, it's just her eyes themselves that don't. But there's no way to know for sure until she heals more."

River smiled indulgently. Natalie wasn't being quite as overbearing as her parents, and was much better about stopping when River asked her too, but it still came up sometimes. Natalie seemed to have a lot more hope than River did at the moment. It was easier for River to just accept that she'd never see again. That this was how life was going to be from now on. Every night before bed she put herself to sleep by running over the images of her favorite things, trying to hold onto every single scrap of detail. The exact shade of Natalie's hair. The color of the sky on a clear July day. The intricate embroidery on the quilt her grandmother had made for her when she turned ten. Those were the things she wanted to focus on, to care about. Not some vague, useless hope for something that felt impossible.

"What about you, Natalie? How have you been?" Dante asked.

She laughed once, though it turned into a sigh as she looked down at the table. "I've spent my whole life taking care of my little siblings, and now they're the ones taking care of me. They set up a little schedule for sleeping on a cot they put in my room, so I'm not alone at night, and they've got all sorts of charts about my medications and recovery timetables for my burns."

"It's adorable, from what I'm told," River said.

"It is," Natalie agreed, managing a quick smile. "I'm so glad I have all three of them."

"My brother's been the same way," Iris said. "I love him, but that kid can hover like nobody's business."

A light chuckle went around the table before silence settled over them, the chatter of the growing crowds around them filling the space.

"Did you hear Toby got transferred to a prison in the city?" Iris asked.

Everyone shook their heads, looking curiously at her.

She sighed. "Yeah, one of the local cops was in for an oil change on his personal car today and told my dad about it. I guess he got beat up pretty bad in the county jail, so they moved him a few days ago."

"Surprised it took that long," Dante said, voice bitter.

Sounds of agreement answered him, though Natalie's had an edge of sadness. She had tried to visit Toby, once, only to be told by his lawyer that Toby was not allowed any visitors that weren't family. She got the distinct impression this was more that Toby was not allowed to visit with anyone else who'd been on the mountain that night.

"They released a new list of charges this morning too," Adam added. "Arson, plus fourteen new charges of manslaughter, and some other little charges."

"I want to believe that'll be enough to put him away," Dante said. "But—"

"But he's an entitled white boy with rich parents," Natalie muttered. She'd been taking what Toby did the hardest.

Some days she thought all this was her fault for being the main reason the others put up with Toby. That if she'd been willing to cut him off for his behavior he wouldn't have been on the camping trip with them, and the fire never would have happened. It had always felt like there was a way to excuse that behavior, though. She'd never been able to see the whole scope of it, and she struggled to even now. Having to stare out at his now empty house across the street every day didn't help either. Toby's parents were supposedly traveling the country to try and put together a team of the fanciest lawyers possible, according to the town rumor mill.

Any further conversation was cut off by the tolling of the church bell. One long, low tone rang out across the town, spreading a hush after it. Dante curled into himself, eyes closing as he swallowed heavily. Iris leaned in to wrap her arms around him, threading her arms carefully to avoid his still healing burns and ribs. Around them everyone was getting up to line the sidewalks and, after a moment, the five of them did as well. Several children with baskets of flowers came down the road, handing out single carnations to everyone, some yellow and some white. Dante's hand shook as he took the yellow one offered to him.

A few blocks away, music began to play, echoing out against the surrounding hills. The somber tones of *Taps* played on bagpipes, backed by a soft medley of drums and other instruments, heralded the arrival of a team of horses pulling onto Main Street from around a corner several blocks down. Aside from Natalie leaning towards River to softly whisper what was happening, the music and oncoming hoofbeats against the asphalt were the only noises.

There were seven horses, one in the lead and the rest in pairs of two behind, all working to pull a long, low trailer. Each of their saddles sat empty, draped in a blanket of yellow carnations. In the trailer were seven empty chairs, draped in white carnations. Behind them trailed the High School band, each member dressed in solid black with a yellow carnation in their lapel and a white one in the band on their black cowboy hats. Bringing up the rear was a collection of retired and off-duty firefighters, all in some sort of uniform.

As the trailer approached where Dante, Iris, Adam, River, and Natalie stood it became apparent that each horse bore a ribbon among their carnations. The six in pairs of two each had the name of a firefighter from Engine 62. All six firefighters had been killed when a burning tree fell and crushed the cab of their engine, preventing any escape. Prior to that, they'd helped rescue at least twelve people.

The horse in the lead did not bear the name of a firefighter. Or at least, it did not bear the name of a man who had started that horrible day as a firefighter. Instead, it read, "Shawn Kristofferson." The man who had descended into the flames in a desperate bid to save his son. The man who, even in the search for his son, had stopped to save others. The man who had perished when his truck succumbed to the heat and fire. His name was the one on that first horse. Upon official confirmation of his death, the local station declared him an honorary firefighter.

Dante, tears streaming down his face now, stood straight backed as he followed the progression of the horses with his eyes. Both of Iris's hands were clasped tightly around one of his. Dante's mother had not come, unable to face such a public memorial.

When the first horse came level with Dante he stepped out onto the street, walking alongside it to tuck his carnation in amongst the others on his father's empty saddle. Once it was secure he continued to walk next to the horse, one hand on its shoulder.

As the procession reached the end of the street the sounds of *Taps* faded away, making room for the church bell to toll once more. Fourteen chimes rolled out, pausing for each to cease before beginning the next.

In Memoriam

Shawn Kristofferson, 48

Engine 62:
David Marshall, 29 • Sarah Williams, 25 • Zane Hayman, 23
Blake Cameron, 36 • Johnny Bridger, 30 • Alex King, 25

The Village:
Alice Heywood, 86 • Marcus Heywood, 89
Alphonse Cox, 12 • Rory Cox, 38 • Lance Mackrel, 24

Newlyweds:
Ronan Gurney, 28 • Sarah Gurney, 27

May they rest in peace.
May their memories be a blessing.

WHERE THEY ARE NOW, FIVE YEARS LATER:

Dante Kristofferson joined a wildland firefighting crew out of Montana and still hopes to join the smokejumpers one day. He and Iris are engaged to be married at the end of the current fire season.

Iris Sawyer used her college fund to start a nonprofit focused on helping queer youth join the rodeo circuit. She currently ranks 3rd in the nation for barrel racing and was able to use her winnings from several post-high school competitions to surgically transition.

River Ashworth received a double eye transplant, but only one took. When she is not home with her wife Natalie, she travels the world to explore everything she can find.

Natalie McLain is pursuing a degree in astrobiology in Washington state. She travels with her wife when her studies allow.

Adam Delgado joined the same wildland firefighting crew as Dante and will be the best man at Dante and Iris's upcoming wedding. He has also published a book of poetry that explores the Lost Hen Fire and its aftereffects, and is pursing a degree in fire science.

Tobias Cassidy pled guilty on all charges, against the wishes of his parents and lawyers. He received a deal for fifty years in prison, with a chance of parole in twenty, a sentence his lawyers and parents have appealed, while many others see it as far too lenient.

AUTHOR NOTE

Growing up in the woods of Colorado, fire is something that has always been a part of my life. When the summer of 2020 came it felt like half the state of Colorado was on fire. Every day there was another one starting somewhere and threatening or destroying places I loved. One even managed to disrupt travel across the whole country by shutting down a major highway for weeks. Two of those fires, the Williams Fork Fire and the East Troublesome Fire, heavily inspired the events of this book, as both were burning very near my home. I spent many days and nights listening to the emergency radio traffic, tracking the fires on my own maps, and doing everything I could to understand what was happening.

These fires gave the book its plot, but they also gave it its helpers, the people who did everything in their power to protect their friends, communities, homes, and total strangers. I wanted to focus on some of those helpers in this book because, despite what Hollywood likes to portray, the world does not turn into an every-man-for-himself hellscape the second things start to go wrong. We deserve to see the everyday helpers just as much as the strong jawed action heroes.

Since that summer, I have gone on to pursue a degree in Wildland Fire Management with a certificate in emergency management, and started working as a wildland fire dispatcher with the Forest Service. I did my best to remain truthful to how the official first responders behave in this book, but there's some things that were changed for the sake of a smooth narrative, especially with the radio chatter. Having a constant, correct usage of the "hey you, its me" format in the calls would've bogged things down, for example. I hope any other professionals reading this book will give me a little grace there!

Please, respect the fire bans. Volunteer to help maintain your local forests. Educate yourself about fire. Make an evacuation plan. Fight for better legislation on climate change and fires.

If you would like to learn more about my work related to disasters, both fiction and non-fiction, please visit my website: www.Katy-L-Wood.com.

Stay safe, and thank you for reading.

DISASTER DISTRESS HOTLINE

If you are in the United States, the Disaster Distress Hotline is a free resource to get mental health support if you have been affected by a disaster, even if you did not go through it yourself. It is confidential, available 24/7, and available in over 100 languages including options for people who are deaf or hard of hearing. It is available via phonecall or text.

1-800-985-5990

OTHER BOOKS BY KATY L. WOOD

Apocalyptic Survival:

Fantasy Adventure: